ELT-DUK AND THE COMPANY OF GOLD HUNTERS

YASH SHARMA

Invincible Publishers

First published in India in 2018

ISBN: 978-93-88333-02-3

Invincible Publishers

G-120, Sushant Lok III, Sector 57, Gurgaon-122002

Registered Address: Opposite Kasturba Ashram, Radaur, Haryana–135133

Printed at Thomson Press (India) LTD

To Lord Shiv,

Lord Parshuraam, a devotee of Lord Shiv (as am I),

He saved mother Earth from the evil many times. I take motivation from them to continue my own journey of life.

To Mother Earth, who gives us love and protection unconditionally, and it is necessary for us to give back to her, whether in the form of love, respect or courage.

Acknowledgement

I am grateful for my hardships and circumstances, a decade long struggle with my work, my health, my mind and the unavoidable situations where I stood alone. I can't express my pain to anyone, but it motivated me to start this beautiful journey. The hand of God (not for football) was clearly over me. He and his guiding spirits helped me a lot through my struggles and I express my gratitude to them. My parents didn't know much about this book till I completed it, but when they found out, they were really happy and surprised, as many others will be when they come to know of it. I thank my parents for how they brought me up and for showering their blessings on me, for which reason I now stand strong. Raghav Sharma, my younger brother, always motivated me and understood my situation well. He holds a special place here for his encouraging words that helped me a lot. My deepest gratitude goes out to all those who helped me in my physical as well as astral form. I write it because I have to write it, and it's my pleasure.

Never doubt yourself. I did before I completed this book, but now I thank myself for having achieved this feat. Thanks to the beautiful soul who motivated me to approach a publisher and helped me through the publishing process which is very tough in itself.

PROLOGUE
ELT-DUK

"Elt-duk" is not just a mountain, but a power center of the Earth too. The mountain always needs a ruler, but it is not easy to rule over Elt-duk as one is first required to win over it. If Elt-duk accepts a ruler, it gives all its powers, lives, and wealth to that ruler. Elt-duk is known for owning great treasures: gold, precious stones, and unaccountable wealth. The ruler of Elt-duk can rule the Earth, with Elt-duk's help of course.

Elt-duk has been here on Earth before the beginning of the first age[1] of Men. It is said that God himself chose to convert Elt-duk from a simple mountain to a stronghold of power. After a long period then, God sent **Als-mites**, otherwise known as 'God's Men', to protect Elt-duk. Many centuries passed, but no one could successfully rule over Elt-duk. At the end of the second age of Men, a brave king from a small kingdom, King Ballanduall, got a chance to rule over Elt-duk due to the bravery he showed against the dark powers and helping Als-mites defeat them.

---

1 An age equals 2000 human years.

Elt-duk gave all its powers and wealth to fulfil the commands of King Ballanduall. But the rule which could have been long led instead to greed, deceit and mutual discord, and eventually got destroyed. Elt-duk was helpless and king-less again.

The Als-mites took charge, but the second age was starting to end and the Als-mites had become weak. Elt-duk needed its new ruler more than ever.

Many stories are associated with Elt-duk regarding God, God's men, and the fights with devils. These stories have continued to grow over time in different ways in different lands. Every kingdom has its own version of the dark stories behind the mystery of Elt-duk. By the third age, stories became myths, people started to believe that Elt-duk was cursed, and that an ancient devil who practised dark magic lived there. It was generally believed that the devil was growing slowly, so everyone was afraid and avoided visiting Elt-duk.

CHAPTER 1

THE TOWN

In one part of Northly Earth, there was a town called Mirkota situated on the banks of river Prancima. It was a happy town that flourished abundantly with nature's gifts. The river Prancima was the soul of the town. With the blessings of the river, the town people produced a huge variety of food products which were largely famous in Northly Earth. People lived in their wooden huts on green and white hummocks. Pavements snaked through the sides of these hummocks to connect the entire town. Each hut owner had a garden in front of the house where one grew flowers and vegetables. The town had many ponds which people used for irrigation and to store water. Mirkota was famous for its bakeries which produced different kinds of bread everyday: cracker (crispy bread), sweet bread with honey, bread ol'apricota (bread of apricot), cheese bread and much more. People loved it. Mirkots also raised cattle. The towners were happy as their business did well. Sometimes, people from the nearby towns came to Mirkota in search of work and food too.

Mirkota's famous carnival, Enchime, took place every year when winter prevailed over Northly Earth. For the festival, the whole town got decorated with lights and glaze paper hanging over the streets, frills everywhere, and shops and houses cleaned and painted with fresh new colours.

Tents were set up over the hummocks with sitting arrangements made for the visitors. Many people from other towns visited, some to see Enchime, while some to make business with their wooden toys and rides. The local people of Mirkota also demonstrate their products at the celebration of Enchime. All of them, whether a towner or a visitor, attended the festival to savour *Gullahony,* a sweetmeat from Mirkota famous across many towns of Northly Earth. It was made from rose milk, rosewater and silver honey from the Belina bee (a bee only found in Mirkota that produced silver coloured honey). Kids, young ones, older ones, everybody relished it equally.

The kids and youngsters especially enjoyed the rides, the firing crackers, and singing the old folk songs of Northly Earth. People sang and danced all evening. Magicians came to show great magic tricks, while the storytellers regaled their listeners with stories of all kinds: magical stories, stories of the beast of Falini, stories of the scary island of Sivaan, and many more. The storytellers' cube would always remain full of kids.

After about thirty to forty days of celebration, Enchime was now about to end for that year. People were tired and the businessmen had done good business with both the locals and the outsiders, and were now all resting in their houses.

There lived some people in the town who didn't like mingling with the other locals. They had been living in Mirkota for many years and if one were to ask a Mirkot what they did, one would receive a variety of answers. They minded their own business. No one knew anything about them.

The **Sword Runner** family lived in Il-dudvar upon the tiny hill. **Tigun Sword Runner** was the leader of the family. He was a tall and strong man with long black hair, a full beard with a few specks of grey in it, and opaque black eyes.

The **Wiser** family lived on Bossing Street near the business centre. **Misarel Wiser** was the main man there, and he mostly lived alone. He was of medium height, had a clean face and short hair.

The **O'blame** family lived in a mansion near Sheyrlpark. **Boreek O'blame** lived there with his wife. He was an old man with no hair on his face, short grey hair on his head and pale green eyes.

These three families were not very friendly with the other Mirkots. They spoke and maintained relations with them only as required. The reason behind this was their line of work. Tigun Sword Runner and Misarel Wiser were partners. Both of them were in their forties. Some called them 'gold hunters', while some knew them as 'soul hunters'. People said they plundered the other lands for wealth. They were gold hunters who hunted for unclaimed wealth of the other lands and the different towns there. O'blame was not their partner. He was an old man in his sixties, but was one of the richest men in all over Northly Earth. He has a large amount of his money invested in several businesses surrounding wood, oil, animals, and herbs. He was a miser and didn't like people much, always suspecting that they would demand money from him.

Happy in their own lives, little did they know how time and situations would bring them all together.

CHAPTER 2

THE COMPANY OF GOLD HUNTERS

It was a quiet and beautiful winter morning. The greenery of Mirkota was covered under the fog of early morning. The lovely chirping of birds could be heard all around. The people of Mirkota were getting ready to start their day. One could smell the aroma of freshly baked bread from the bakeries of the town. Gradually, people started to gather at the meeting points in the markets for their daily dose of discussions, tea and breakfast with their friends and relatives.

The whiff of fresh brewing tea and breakfast soaked the air of the Sword Runners' residence too. The place was abuzz with the daily morning activities. The women of the house prepared tea and sweet bread with butterball for everyone, while Tigun Sword Runner sat with his elder brother, Holbaat Sword Runner, in the garden out front. Their house was a tall stone building with pale white paint on it. It had bright blue doors, while the garden extending from it flourished with several colourful flowers. It had been adorned with a garden table and some chairs.

Tigun had returned home just a month ago from his not-so-successful mission. While Tigun regularly went out for hunts, Holbaat stayed back with the family and took command of the house. Tigun was not happy with his last mission. He was sharpening his sword while drinking tea with Holbaat. Holbaat asked him about his future missions, but he just mumbled in response uninterestedly. On their last mission, Holbaat's son Momunsha had gotten injured badly. Tigun had been deeply affected by it and didn't wish to talk about hunts for a while.

While they were drinking tea and having breakfast, they suddenly heard a loud voice coming from outside their house. "Open the door"—tap, tap— "Open the door!"

"Misarel?" Tigun called out.

"YES," the voice replied.

Aziredun, Tigun's younger son, went to open the door and Misarel Wiser, Tigun's hunting partner, entered the house, with a pigeon perched on his shoulder. They hunted for gold and wealth through the other lands and various towns of Northly Earth.

"What happened? Where have you been since last month?" Tigun asked.

"Something important and urgent came up, that's why I have come here now," Misarel said. Tigun, Holbaat and Misarel walk a little farther away from the others.

"I have good news," Misarel said excitedly.

"What is it?" Tigun asked.

"Ispichu has arrived with golden news," Misarel said.

"What kind of golden news?" Holbaat asked. Ispichu was a well-trained communicator pigeon whose speciality was that he could travel with lightning fast speed. Ispichu was a unique pigeon who had a patch of red fur at the centre of its forehead that made him look distinctive.

Usually, Ispichu travelled with Tigun and Misarel, but before their last mission, Misarel had sent Ispichu to Elt-duk. Misarel had known that it was too risky to send Ispichu there, but he was the only and the best communicator he had. Misarel had an inkling that something odd was happening there, and wanted to investigate. That's why he had sent Ispichu, but Tigun didn't know about it.

"From where has Ispichu arrived with the golden news ?" Tigun asked.

"I had sent him to Elt-duk,"Misarel replied.

"What?!" Tigun and Holbaat exclaimed in shock and surprise. "Why, why would you send Ispichu there?"

"What's on your mind, Misarel? Elt-duk is a dark and dangerous place. It is cursed. You know this, we all know it. Then why did you send Ispichu there?" Holbaat asked, worried.

"I know…I know, the place is dangerous, but something very odd is happening there," Misarel broke his silence.

"What is happening there?" Tigun asked.

"I heard about the blaze of Elt-duk. We all have heard about it. Almost a year ago when we were hunting in Rovanta, we met with some monks. They were coming from Buk-din-duk, do you remember? Did you know that?" Misarel asked quickly.

Tigun nodded his head in response, although he didn't remember much about it. He just muttered a *Hmm* and Misarel took a long breath.

"So, what's in it?" Holbaat asked Misarel.

Misarel sat on a chair, while Aziredun came to them with fresh cups of tea, butterball and sweet bread. The air between them carried silence for a while as Aziredun came in. Misarel took a sip of his tea with a bite of the sweet bread placed before him. As soon as Azirdun was well out of ear-shot, he starts talking, "One of the monks had told me that the darker side of Elt-duk was glowing, that he had seen the blaze of Elt-duk himself."

"What rubbish!" Holbaat intervened.

"It is true," Misarel said confidently.

"How are you so sure?" Tigun asked.

Misarel put his hand in his pocket and took out a gold coin from it.

"What is that?" Tigun asked upon noticing that the coin was glowing.

Misarel smiled and said, "This, my friend, is the gold of Elt-duk. Take it." He handed it over to Tigun.

"It is hot," Tigun whispered.

"Yes. It is from the blaze of Elt-duk," said Misarel.

Holbaat took the coin.

"Whose face is engraved on it?" Tigun asked Misarel.

"I don't know, maybe some King," Misarel replied.

"How did you get it?" Holbaat asked.

"The monk gave it to me, he is free from greed. When I asked him for it, he agreed to give me one. He told me that the blaze of Elt-Duk will start shortly and that it will spew out uncountable gold and wealth. I was skeptical about it too, so when we returned to Mirkota after the hunt of Rovanta, I trained Ispichu for Elt-duk. Actually, I was not sure if Ispichu would manage to return, but he did and with such golden news. You can ask Ispichu yourself, Tigun," Misarel said.

Tigun and Misarel understood Ispichu's language as they had trained him themselves. Tigun asked Ispichu what he knew about the blaze of Elt-duk, and Ispichu told him everything.

It was then that Tigun finally came to believe Misarel, while Holbaat still remained confused and doubtful. Their conversation ended with the tea, butterball and breads. Tigun and Misarel decided to meet the next day at Graping's Goon, a local restaurant. This place was older than a century and was considered the pride of Mirkota. Its interiors had an antique charm to it, with old wooden furniture and dim lights.

The next day, Tigun reached the place early and ordered a pint of Gring (a local beer) for himself with a side of mashed potatoes and corchetta cheese. Tigun looked eager as he waited desperately for Misarel. He kept thinking about Elt-duk. When Misarel arrived, Tigun stood up and called out, "Misarel!"

"Yes, my friend," Misarel said as he approached Tigun and put his hand on his shoulder. Tigun ordered another pint of Gring for Misarel. Gulping it down together, they started talking about the rumoured blaze of Elt-duk.

"How do we start?" Tigun asked Misarel, looking straight into his eyes.

"It will be a much bigger hunt than usual," Misarel said.

“Yes,” Tigun replied. “Would just the two of us be able to complete this hunt?”

“We need at least one more partner, someone who is financially strong,” Misarel said.

“Where will we find someone who is financially strong? The rich people of Mirkota don’t like us,” Tigun said, crestfallen.

“Don’t worry, my friend, we can manage one,” Misarel said, positively.

“Who?” Tigun asks with curiosity.

“O’blame.”

“What? That old man? Is he even interested in us, in our missions? Since when?”

“I can handle him,” Misarel said confidently.

“But he is a miser. Why would he be even remotely interested in our hunt?” Tigun asked.

“His businesses are down these days. The flame of Corga[1] adversely affected his wood and forest related businesses. Many investors are now demanding their money back from him. He once asked me about our work and offered that I visit his house for a meeting. Despite the losses, he has got enough to finance our hunt, but is also seeking a new business opportunity to multiply his wealth,” Misarel explained.

“But I have also heard he is not a good man. He is miserly and greedy,” Tigun said, caressing the worry lines that had furrowed his forehead.

“We don’t have much time, Tigun. If we start searching for another investor now, it would take a long time. There is

1 Corga was a dense forest with a huge expanse

very less chance that someone here would be ready to invest in a gold hunt with us, since everyone hates us," Misarel said in one breath.

"Hmm..."

"You don't want to go on this hunt?" Misarel asked.

"Yes, I want to. I don't have a choice and I don't have any other work," Tigun replied exasperatedly. "We should meet Boreek O'blame then. We will also need food and supplies, a bigger ship, more men, and more money. Just the two of us won't be able to gather the resources required for this hunt, as we do not have that much money and...wealth, the wealth is uncountable as you know."

Tigun understood the situation. He had to go for this hunt, which meant that they needed money, and money could only come from one source, their only hope–Mr. Boreek O'blame. Tigun and Misarel drowned their pints and got ready to set up a meeting with O'blame. While leaving Graping's Goon, they decided to fix a meeting with O'blame at his house for the next evening. They were desperate to convince him into investing his money in their hunt.

The next evening, Tigun and Misarel reached O'blame's house. O'blame lived in a posh mansion near Sheyrlpark. Tigun and Misarel got down from their horses and left them to graze at the paddock. There was a big garden in front of the house. They stepped into the foyer and called a servant, "Tell Mr O'blame, Tigun and Misarel have arrived."

The servant asked them to wait in the sitting area. They nodded and went to the place where they had been directed by the servant. It was a big hall with some old paintings hanging on the walls. There was a table with a flower vase on it, and the rest of the furniture was minimal. Everything had dull colours. They seated themselves on a big puffed sofa placed in the middle.

"He is a miser, what can one expect from him?" Tigun exclaimed, looking around the room.

"Shh...he is coming!" Misarel whispered.

'Hello Misarel, how are you?" O'blame asked Misarel, shaking hands with him and Tigun. "Sit," he instructed.

"We have come here with a business opportunity, sir," Misarel said.

"What kind of a business, Misarel? Hunt of gold? Haha," he asked with a cruel laugh. "You call that business?"

"Yes,"Misarel replied confidently.

"It's a crime, not business," O'blame accused. On hearing this, Tigun stood up in fury and strutted towards O'blame. O'blame became frightened by the look of anger in Tigun's eyes and looked around for help. Small beads of sweat start forming on his forehead. Misarel grabbed Tigun's hand and urged him to sit back down.

"I mean, it is not a business," O'blame said. "Why should I get involved in this?"

Tigun began to think that the deal would not come to fruition. But then, Misarel started explaining. "Yes sir, it is a business. We hunt in different lands, but we hunt only for the gold which is not claimed by any man or King. We do it without causing harm to any other people."

"What about the weapons you carry?" O'blame interrupted.

"The weapons are for our safety," Misarel replied.

"Hmm, so where are you going hunting next and what do you want from me?" O'blame asked boldly.

"We are embarking upon the biggest hunt of our times soon and we need you to invest in it. In return, you shall get an equal share in profit,"Misarel replied.

"Why equal? I want a larger share than both of you since I will have invested more than you two," O'blame answered greedily. Tigun looked at Misarel with a helpless expression on his face.

"Sir, we will give you the opportunity of coming on the hunt with us. We have men who are experienced with such kind of hunts, men who are ready to work hard, who can fight for us. Both Tigun and I know the places and the people who live in all corners of the world. Thus, we shall share the profits equally," Misarel replied calmly.

"Quite smart!" O'blame said. "But you didn't tell me where you are planning to go hunting."

"Elt-duk," Tigun replied. Misarel gave Tigun a hard look, gesturing why he had revealed it to him all so soon.

"What?" O'blame sat up in surprise.

"The blaze of Elt-duk has started. Not a lot of people know about it still and we can take it to our advantage," Misarel said.

"I don't want to go to Elt-duk. It is risky and is too far from here. I have heard many bad stories about that place right from my childhood. All of them are scary," O'blame said nervously.

"Yes, it is far and it is risky. That is why such a huge amount of gold there has remained untouched and unclaimed till now. It is waiting for us," Misarel replied confidently.

"How are you so sure about it?" O'blame asked after contemplating the proposal silently.

"About what?" Misarel asks.

"About the uncountable gold."

Misarel smiled, realizing that O'blame was now in his hands. "Yes sir, the uncountable gold is indeed at the mountain," he said, pointing his finger up. "Do you want to see a sample of the blaze of Elt-duk?" Misarel took out the gold coin and showed it to O'blame.

The greed for gold reflected clear in O'blame's eyes. "Is it real?"

"Yes," Misarel replied.

"It is hot, why is it hot?" O'blame asked.

"It has come out of the blaze of Elt-duk."

"Who is this man on the coin?" O'blame asked again.

"I don't know," Misarel replied and took the coin from O'blame. "What do you think about the hunt, sir?" he asked softly.

"I can't give an answer now. I will take some time to think over it…"

"Sir, I know you have lost many businesses. Many of your investors want their money back. If you stay here, you'd have to pay your debts. Why don't you join us immediately? If you come with us, your money's worth will increase a hundred times over," Misarel said, hoping to tempt O'blame. "Give us your answer soon. We will not wait for long; we have to arrange things for the hunt soon."

Their meeting ended with this discussion.

After the meeting, Tigun and Misarel went back to their horses. While leaving, Tigun asked Misarel if he thought O'blame would join them. "He will join us tomorrow," Misarel replied confidently.

The next morning, Tigun reached Misarel's house which was near Mirkota's business center. It was a big stone house has a wooden entrance gate. There was a paddock near the gate where some horses stood grazing. Misarel lived alone there. His family lived separately near the town. Behind Misarel's house, there was a small stone building, the way to which went through the corridor that lay in front of the main door. This was Misarel's office. Tigun sat there waiting for Misarel. A servant came in with some tea and crackers for Tigun. He sipped his tea while thinking about the future, about O'blame's decision, and how they would manage everything. Would O'blame say yes? Pondering over all this, he drowned his tea.

He heard a voice just then, coming from outside the door, "Tigun, my friend, you have arrived!" Misarel was at the door. He came closer and hugged him. Another person entered the office behind him, it was O'blame.

"Mr O'blame is ready to join us, Tigun," Misarel said loudly and happily. Tigun's eyes widened in surprise.

"Really?" Tigun asked.

"Yes, my friend. Yes."

Tigun took a step forward towards O'blame, and O'blame took a step back, remembering the fury in Tigun's eyes from the previous evening. Tigun shook O'blame's hand warmly and thanked him. Misarel ordered the servant to bring in a bottle of Blime (a luxurious wine made from limunberry fruit and aged for many years).

The servant came back with Blime, opened the bottle and poured it into three glasses. He also brought with it crisp potatoes with spicy corn and cheese. Misarel gave a glass of wine to O'blame and Tigun each. Tigun refused as he had just had tea. "Oh, forget the tea, take a sip. Today is our day, Tigun," Misarel insisted joyously.

They started discussing the hunt. Agreements were made and all the partners signed it after some days with the hope of getting the expected fruitful results.

CHAPTER 3

PREPARING FOR THE HUNT

It was decided that Tigun would go to Glosaang, a village a month's man-sprint away from Mirkota, to recruit some strong men for the hunt.

Misarel, on the other hand, started the process of making the biggest ship that they had ever made. With the help of Holbaat, weapons like swords, spears, shields, armguards, chest guards, bows, and arrows etc. were prepared.

As O'blame had many businesses, he was given the responsibility to procure food and supplies, useful medical herbs, horses, etc. for the journey.

The trio was ready to start their work as decided.

Early morning the next day, Tigun took his best horse, Doro, and left Mirkota with some necessarily things. The journey was long and tiring. On his way, Tigun was to cross the town of Moneka where he could rest for a day or two, then continue his journey towards Mugaan, a lonely town. Very few people resided in Mugaan, and those who lived there were not very friendly. After crossing Moneka, Tigun rested in Mugaan for a day, and the next destination was the town of Glosaang.

Glosaang did not have many wealthy people, or provide very good business opportunities. Brown trees with white shade, called Gleekwood trees, were everywhere. Gleekwood was the symbol of the town. It was famous for its strong wood, but the town couldn't take advantage of it very well.

Tigun had last visited Glosaang a year ago. He noticed now that the town was starting to change. He went to Mojin's inn. Tigun and Glosaang shared a very unique relationship. A couple of years ago, when Tigun and Misarel were on a hunt, Tigun fell from Doro and got injured while they were crossing Glosaang. They decided to stay in Glosaang till Tigun became healthier again. They stayed at Mojin's inn. A lot of towners came to see them, as they didn't know much about other towns or people from outside their own little establishment. Kids looked at them with curiosity and Misarel told them many interesting stories. The kids loved Misarel's stories.

Doperi Thilmus was an elderly man of the village who possessed great knowledge about medicinal herbs and used them to take care of Tigun. He was always seen wearing a white shirt and brown pants with a black waist coat over his white shirt. He was a wise old man. He told them the story of a beast called Sharptooth, a large tiger-like beast with sharp teeth, golden eyes and powerful agility with which he could kill any man in a second, slashing them fatally with his sharp tooth. Both Misarel and Tigun were curious to know more. They asked him if the stories about Sharptooth were true.

Doperi took a long breath and said, "They are true and Sharptooth is unfortunately real. He lives in Corga and often comes to Glosaang to hunt. Sharptooth has killed many people of this town, that's why this town is so unpleasant. There used to be great wealth in this town before. He snatched all our happiness and freedom from us. We are cursed." Doperi got emotional towards the end.

“This is not good at all. You people should fight against him together,” Tigun said angrily.

“We tried, but failed. Many of our youth died while fighting. It’s worthless.”Saying this, Doperi gave the herbs to Tigun and left.

“This is cruel, Misarel. How can a mere beast, an animal, spoil a whole town? He is a beast. Something needs to be done here,”Tigun said.

“Hmm,” Misarel replied.

After some days, Tigun found himself completely healed. They planned to resume their hunt and prepared to leave. Doperi came to see them off. “Thanks Doperi,” Tigun expressed his gratitude towards him as they were leaving.

“No, it was my duty,” Doperi replied pleasantly.

“You took care of us as if you’ve know us for a long time,” Misarel said. “Thanks again.” Suddenly, they heard a roar resounding round the town. “Sharptooth has arrived,” Doperi said with fear. “He is hungry, he will kill all of us.” He trembled with fear.

“We should get out of here,” Misarel said to Tigun.

“Go!” Doperi said. “Save your life.”

“But we can’t leave you here all helpless,” Tigun replied.

“Nothing will happen to me. You two, go and protect yourself. Take the outer pavements of Glosaang, go!” Doperi instructed urgently.

They mounted their horses and started galloping towards the outer pavement of the town. Suddenly, Tigun saw the beast entering the town.

Tall and bulky, the beast seemed to be almost three times the size of any man. His skin was pale yellow with dark black stripes. Tigun pointed him out to Misarel. "We should move fast," Misarel said, but Tigun suddenly saw Sharptooth approaching the kids who often used to come to Mojin's Inn to listen to Misarel's stories. They had all become good friends with Tigun too. Tigun turned Doro in their direction and urged him to run faster.

"What you doing, Tigun?" Misarel screamed.

"I know those kids, Misarel...we have to save them."

On hearing this, Misarel turned his horse too.

As Sharptooth approached the kids, a heavy stone hit his head and he winced with pain.

"Here," Tigun shouted. When he saw Tigun, his golden eyes got filled with rage.

"Take the kids, Misarel, and call the towners!"

As Sharptooth stepped towards Tigun, Misarel grabbed the kids and ran the opposite way. Tigun pulled his sword out of its sheath as Sharptooth pounced at him. Tigun dodged, but fell down from Doro. Sharptooth jumped at him many times, but Tigun continued to dodge each time. Tigun knew that Sharptooth was hungry and hurt, so he decided to tire him out as much as possible before making his attack. When Sharptooth jumped at him again, he managed to inflict a cut on his face with his sword. Sharptooth broke a tooth from the impact. It made him all the more angry, and he attacked Tigun again. Amidst all the dodges, Tigun somehow managed to hit Sharptooth almost four times more with his sword. Many towners had arrived along with Misarel by then. All became witness to the glorious battle being fought between Tigun and Sharptooth. While dodging Sharptooth, Tigun grabbed a big stone and threw it towards Sharptooth's face. It hit him bang in the middle and knocked him unconscious.

It was a victory!

The people of the town clapped and cheered, then approached Tigun and lifted him up on their shoulders while chanting his name loudly. Tigun became their hero as he had defeated Sharptooth, Glosaang's biggest threat. The entire town celebrated the victory with food, dance, and wine. From that day onwards, Tigun got a new name from them: **Sharptooth**. The tooth which had fallen from the beast Sharptooth's mouth now hung around his neck.

After that day, Sharptooth never came back to Glosaang. It is said that he went back to Corga and never returned.

Many years after that day, when Tigun arrived at Mojin's Inn, the owner welcomed him warmly. When the kids saw him, they screamed, "Sharptooth has arrived! Sharptooth has arrived!" Some people got frightened upon hearing the name of the beast, and asked their kids worriedly, "Where? Where?"

"At Mojin's Inn," the kids replied, pointing towards Tigun who had just entered the Inn.

"What business brings you here, Mr. Tigun?" the owner asked.

"Serious business," Tigun replied. "But first, I will rest tonight."

"Sure, sir."

The next day, Tigun went to Doperi Thilmus' house and explained to him the reason for his visit. Doperi and Tigun start looking for lads to take on the hunt. News of this recruitment spread all over town. The selection process ran for about two or three days. Doperi and Tigun picked out almost a hundred young men, all of whom were strongly built. Some of them knew a good deal about ships and its mechanisms, while some were good cooks, and the others were warriors. Tigun then described the hunt to them, the place they had planned to go to, and what share they would all get after the hunt.

After all of them left, Tigun asked Doperi if they would join him. Doperi remained quiet for sometime, then said, “Maybe they will join you because they respect you, maybe they won’t because of Elt-duk, since it is so far and risky.”

They went to Doperi’s house after. Doperi’s wife had made tea for them. Tigun took a sip and asked Doperi, “When will you come with the lads then?”

“What do you mean?” Doperi asked, widening his eyes in surprise.

“I mean, you are their leader. You will have to come with them,” Tigun answered.

“But you didn’t ask me this before,”Doperi replied.

“No, I am not asking. I know you will come with them.”

“How on earth did you believe that I would come with you? And…and for Elt-duk no less? Never!” Doperi said.

“You are necessary for us. You have to come for us, Doperi. You are the only one in the whole of Northly Earth who knows all the herbs and their uses so well.”

“Don’t try to flatter me,” Doperi replied.

“I am not flattering you. I need you, we need you. Please Doperi, have a heart. You have to come.”

Doperi didn’t answer.

"Alright then, I will not force you. But if you do decide to come, you are most welcome and we shall be very pleased to have you. Take this."

"What is this?" Doperi asked.

"A sack of gold coins and the agreement for the hunt. Give the coins to the lads or their parents as a token and tell them that I am taking their children on a mission and that I will take care of them."

"When you will leave Glosaang?"Doperi asked.

"Tomorrow."

*****

During these days, Misarel was actively working on building the ship and armours in Mirkota, while O'blame had arranged for the money and supplies.

Tigun returned to Mirkota from his long journey to Glosaang after about twenty days. A servant gave the news of Tigun's return to Misarel.

"Go and tell him that I will come meet him tomorrow morning," Misarel instructed the servant.

While drinking tea the next morning, Tigun asked Holbaat about the preparations for the hunt. Holbaat gave Tigun all the details about weapons, the ship, food and supplies, etc. After some time, there was a knock on the door, "Tigun, Tigun."

"Come Misarel," Tigun replied from inside. Misarel entered and sat next to Tigun. "How was the journey to Glosaang?" Misarel asked.

"Fine," Tigun replied while making tea.

"Did it not work out like we had thought?" Misarel asked again.

"I did my best, selected almost a hundred lads, gave them the token amount too, but you know, everyone is frightened of Elt-duk," Tigun answered.

"What about Doperi? Can't he bring the lads with him?"

Tigun said nothing.

"Why are you silent, Tigun?"

"I think he might not come, but I still hope," Tigun replied.

"What are you saying, Tigun? He is very necessary for us, for this hunt. If he does not agree to it, how will the other lads come? Besides, we don't have anyone else who knows how to treat sick and injured people!"

"He will come," Tigun replied.

"I should have gone there instead of you," Misarel said in anger. He stood up and left Tigun's house, feeling hopeless. Tigun felt worried for Doperi and his lads.

The next day, Tigun and Misarel went to O'blame's house together, but he was not there. A servant told them that he had gone to the White-ord (the river bank of Prancima). The place had been named White-ord after Mirkota's first Captain's wife, Lady Crasey Ord. She had planted a thousand white lilies on the banks of Prancima almost a century ago, and they were still there. The flowers added great charm to the place. Mirkota's port had also been built on the same bank, which received and departed many merchant and traveller ships.

Tigun and Misarel made their way down to White-ord to meet O'blame. Misarel told him about Tigun's journey to Glosaang and what all had happened there.

"You should have gone there, Misarel," O'blame said.

"I know, Mr. O'blame. I feel the same."

While O'blame and Misarel were talking, Tigun surveyed the ship keenly. "The ship is coming out nicely. Almost everything has been completed here."

"Yes...food, herbs, weapons, everything is arranged. We only need the lads now," Misarel taunted.

"Which means, our mission is going to end even before it starts," O'blame said.

"No," Tigun said loudly. "The hunt will not end. It will start."

"But how?" O'blame asked.

"Do not worry about it. Just be prepared, we will start our hunt in thirty days," declared Tigun.

All of them left White-ord feeling uncertain and anxious.

The investment was done. It was now necessary for them to start the hunt, but they still lacked the manpower.They knew no Mirkots who'd be ready to go with them on this hunt.

CHAPTER 4

MOMUNSHA'S HEALTH

That night, Tigun went to Momunsha's room. Momunsha was Holbaat's son. He was a brave warrior who accompanied Tigun and Misarel on their hunts and helped them. He had gotten badly injured on their last hunt. Tigun sat beside Momunsha's bed and asked, "How's your wound now?"

"Not okay yet, still in pain," Holbaat, who was also in the room, said. "He has broken the bone in his right arm. It still has not adjusted."

"Do you drink Quetish[2] regularly?" Tigun asked.

"Yes," Momunsha replied. Momunsha's wife came in right then with food and some Quetish. Holbaat and Tigun came out of Momunsha's room.

"How will Momunsha come on this hunt with us? He is badly injured and I can't risk taking him to Elt-duk in this condition," Tigun said, while Holbaat remained silent. "You know, Holbaat, Momunsha is a great warrior. His skills are unmatched. He is trustworthy."

"I fear for him whenever he goes with you on the hunts," Holbaat broke his silence.

---

2 A drink made from herbs that is effective in adjusting broken bones and mitigating pain.

"We need him, this hunt needs him, but how do I take him like this? I don't think he will be able to go," Tigun said worriedly.

Momunsha still didn't know anything about this hunt to Elt-duk, and Tigun asked Holbaat not to tell him anything about it.

The next day, Misarel and Tigun meet at Graping's Goon again. They ordered two pints of gring.

"Are they coming?" Misarel asked.

"Yes," Tigun replied confidently.

"You are bluffing, Tigun. At least, don't lie to me. Hundreds of Droshes[3] have already been invested. We are on a deadline. O'blame is not in the mood to start anymore and is now asking us to return his money. I have somehow pacified him for the moment. How will we do this, Tigun?"

Tigun remained quiet. While they shared an anxious silence, voices of happy Mirkots drinking their pints of gring filled the Goon.

"How's Momunsha now?" Misarel asked.

"Not okay. His broken bone has not adjusted properly still."

Misarel put his hand over his head and took a deep breath.

"How will we start, Tigun? I don't understand what is happening. Momunsha is a well trained warrior and an important counterpart for us. This hunt requires him. Is he really hurt, or do you and Holbaat just don't want to take him to Elt-duk?"

---

3 A drosh is a sack of 1000 coins

"What you saying, Misarel? Do you think we would ever think like this? Momunsha got injured on our last hunt. He still doesn't know anything about this hunt or Elt-duk. If he comes to know about it, he will insist on coming with us despite his injury."

Silence hung in the air between them again. After some more discussion, they left Graping's Goon.

Early morning the next day, Misarel visited Tigun's house. He still thought that Tigun had been lying about Momunsha. Without informing or knocking at the main gate, he quietly entered into the corridor to reach the verandah in the middle of the house. All the rooms in the house had been built around this space.

"Where is Momunsha?" he asked a servant. The servant indicated Momunsha's room to him. Misarel rapidly went over to stand beside Momunsha's bed. He watched him for some time, the wooden band on his arm and the Quetish in a clay glass on his table.

"Momunsha," Misarel spoke slowly.

"Who's it?" Momunsha asked.

"Misarel. How are you, Momunsha? How's your arm now?"

"Not good, it is still hurting. I feel very bad here. I felt like a caged animal. Are you and uncle not planning any hunt anytime soon? I want to come with you."

"You are not well, Momunsha. You should rest," Misarel replied.

In the meantime, the servant went to Tigun and told him that Misarel had come and was with Momunsha in his room. Tigun made his way over to Momunsha's room too.

"Uncle," Momunsha said as he saw Tigun enter. Misarel turned around to face him.

"When did you come, Misarel?" Tigun asked.

"I came just now to see Momunsha."

Tigun understood that Misarel hadn't believed him the previous night.

"Take care, Momunsha," Misarel said and came out into the corridor with Tigun.

"Sorry," Misarel said.

"Why?" Tigun asked.

"I didn't believe you yesterday."

"Yes, you didn't."

Both of them walked out of the house, talking about the problems they were facing and how they would deal with them. Just then, Tigun's elder son, Asto, came home and greeted his father and Misarel. He had been out of Mirkota for a few days.

"How are you, Asto?" Misarel asked.

"I am fine," he said and entered the house.

"What is he doing nowadays?" Misarel asked Tigun.

"Nothing much," Tigun replied.

"Why?" Misarel asked.

"I don't know what he wants, he doesn't talk to me a lot," Tigun replied.

"And what about you? Do you talk?"

"Not much," Tigun replied.

"Oh, you should talk to him. He is growing up to be a young man. Does he have any interest in our hunts?" Misarel asked.

"I don't know. But how can we take him? He is not experienced at all and Elt-duk is a dangerous place for a novice like him," Tigun replied.

"You should ask him if he is interested. He can be trained, and he is your son. I am sure he has your qualities. Ask him, Tigun," Misarel said and left.

Chapter 5

Arrival of Asto

Asto was a tall, fair, and intelligent young man in his twenties. He had long curly black hair and a pretty smile. Being a Sword Runner, he was a born warrior and knew swordplay quite well, though he had not been tested yet. He had travelled out of Mirkota for two years because of some work he want to do, but did not succeed. He had come back the previous year and had been living in Mirkota since then without doing much. He asked Tigun about his hunts sometimes, but never got any substantive answers. He was frustrated with his hard luck and terrible situation. He also did not like to share his problems with anyone.

As he entered the house, he proceeded directly to Momunsha's room.

"How are you, Momu?" he asked.

"Not good at all," Momunsha replied, and they both laughed.

Asto took a seat beside him and started, "Tell me more about the hunt of Klava. You didn't tell me about the biggest fish. Did you see it?"Asto asked.

"Yes, I did."

"Really? How big was it?"

"Almost triple the size of us," Momunsha replied. Asto's eyes widened to triple their capacity.

"What about the smiley monkey? Does he really smile?"

"Yes…yes, always."

They laughed again.

"Momunsha, have you ever killed anyone?"Asto asked.

"No," Momunsha replied. "We fight only to defend ourselves."

"I would defend myself if you take me on a hunt. Then I will show you." Asto motioned his hands to convince Momunsha.

Tigun was standing right outside Momunsha's room and was listening to everything. He realised that Asto was indeed interested in hunts and in all that they did. He thought of all the pros and cons of having Asto with them on this hunt, then went back to his own room, while Asto and Momunsha continued talking.

Tigun and Misarel went to White-ord every day to check on their ship.

"Not many days are left now, Tigun," Misarel said. "Did you speak to Asto?"

"No," Tigun replied.

"What golden moment are you waiting for?"

"None, but I do think that he is interested in our hunts. He was talking to Momunsha about our hunts the other day."

"Then why are we waiting? We should take him with us, Tigun. I will talk to him and train him in whatever days that are left before we leave."

Back at his house, Tigun summoned Asto to him. "Do you have any knowledge or interest in our hunts?"

"Yes," Asto stammered.

"Do you know anything about our hunts?"

"A little bit."

"Good. Uncle Misarel has asked you to come to White-ord with me."

"Why?" Asto asked.

"I will tell you there," said Tigun and went to his room.

Asto was still confused why his father had asked him these things, because he was not very conversational with him otherwise.

The next morning, Tigun asked his wife, "Where is Asto?"

"I am ready, Pa," Asto said, hurrying out of his room.

Tigun smiled at him. "Let's go."

Both Asto and Tigun headed down to White-ord where Misarel was waiting for them. Asto greeted Misarel upon seeing him.

"Hello, younger Tigun. How are you?"

"I am good," Asto replied beaming.

"May I ask you something?" Misarel said. "Do you like this ship?"

"Yes, it is beautiful. Are you going on a hunt again?" Asto asked.

"Yes, do you want to come with us?" Misarel asked quickly. Asto became silent and looked at Tigun.

"We are indeed going on a hunt, Asto, and this is going to be your father's biggest hunt yet," Misarel explained.

"Oh, okay," Asto replied.

"But don't reveal this to anyone, not even Momunsha," Misarel warned. "Tell me, Asto, do you like hunts and adventures?" he asked.

"I don't know yet," Asto replied. He felt confused because Tigun had also asked him the same question the previous day.

"Okay. No problem. But I know you like our hunts."

"How do you know that?" Asto asked.

"Momunsha told me that you love listening to the stories of our adventures and hunts from him. Am I right, Asto?"

Asto remained silent, but there was a little smile on his face.

"You know, Asto, your brother Momunsha is a great warrior. He has saved many lives and has fought with many men and beasts."

"What kind of beasts?" Asto asked.

"Oh! The beast of Falini and the beast of Hovel woods."

Somehow, Tigun knew that Asto was sinking into what Misarel was doing. He was doing what he was best at, making up Asto's mind. "We encounter many beasts on our hunts, and there are so many places that you would surely like to see, Asto," Misarel said. "Would you like to join us from tomorrow? We can start your training for the hunt. I know you are doing nothing as such nowadays, so why don't you join us?"

Asto looked at Tigun, then silently replied, "Okay," after sometime.

"You may go now. Your father will stay here. Be sure to come tomorrow morning," instructed Misarel.

After Asto left, Tigun expressed his worries to Misarel, "Would it really be okay to take him to Elt-duk? It is a dangerous place and he knows nothing about our hunts."

"Why are you so worried, Tigun? I know he is not experienced, but we need a replacement for Momunsha, and Asto is our best bet! Also, we are here for him. We will teach him everything. He is your son, Tigun. He will learn quickly, don't worry. He is a very nice boy, Tigun. You are lucky."

They entered the ship to see if everything was ready.

All the preparations on the ship had been done, the weapons were ready, the food and supplies were stored properly. All that was left to do was to just wait for Doperi and his lads.

The next morning, Asto arrived at White-ord as per schedule. Misarel was there already. "Come Asto!" Misarel shouted.

As he reached the dock, Misarel handed him a sword. "Grab this firmly and try to defend yourself. Don't be frightened."

Asto smiled. Misarel attacked him but he dodged it and defended himself well.

"Very nice, Asto! Do you know swordplay?" Misarel asked eagerly.

"Momunsha taught me. We practice when he returns after hunts," Asto answered.

"Then you must know how to attack too. Attack me."

Asto did as directed.

"Very nice! Very good, Asto. You are indeed good at swordplay, but your father is the real master of weapons. I don't think you need any beginner's lessons. Come with me, I will teach you about ships and map reading."

Asto was happy to learn all these new things and was excited to know that he was going on a hunt with them. He still didn't know the place where they were going, but he didn't bother to ask. Many years of idleness and failure had taught him to take happily whatever came in his stride. He didn't know whether this hunt would turn out to be good or bad, he just accepted it.

After a couple of days, O'blame called Misarel and Tigun to his house. "Are we going on the hunt or not?" he asked in frustration.

"Yes, we are," they replied.

"Where are the lads?" O'blame asked.

"They are coming," Tigun replied. Misarel looked at Tigun in an uncertain manner.

"I don't think they are coming, and this mission will end before it even begins," O' blame said, sounding quite frustrated again.

"I will not let this mission end, Mr. O'blame. I will arrange for men from elsewhere if those from Glosaang do not come," Tigun replied in anger.

"And I trust Tigun. If he says they are coming, then they are definitely coming," supported Misarel.

When Tigun and Misarel left O'Blame's house after the meeting, Misarel asked, "Are they really coming, Tigun?"

"Yes they are," Tigun replied.

Days were getting less colder now. Asto's training continued on. He came to know that they were going to Elt-duk from the books and maps that he studied on the ship.

Early one morning, Tigun arrived at Misarel house. "Misarel," he shouted loudly.

"Yes?"

"Come over here!"

"What happened? You look like you are in a hurry," Misarel said from upstairs.

"Ispichu has come back," Tigun said.

"From where?" Misarel asked in surprise as he came down. "Where had you sent Ispichu?"

"I had sent him to Glosaang with a message for Doperi almost twenty days ago and it worked! Ispichu has returned with a message from Glosaang."

"What is the message?" Misarel enquired excitedly.

"Doperi is coming with the lads. They will reach here in about a week," Tigun answered.

"Good lord! That is great news, Tigun!" Misarel started to dance in his room, singing his favourite folk songs of Northly Earth. "You are great, Tigun. We can start our hunt now. I knew you could do it. We should go to O'blame's house and tell him the good news."

CHAPTER 6

THE PARTY BEGINS

Asto had now grown familiar with swordplay and map reading. Everyone spent most of their time at the White-ord shipyard where their ship was docked with all its weapons and supplies for the hunt. Asto didn't talk to O'blame, unless when absolutely necessary.

A week had passed and Doperi was to arrive with his lads in Mirkota any moment as per Ispichu's message. Misarel sent Asto with some other men to the entrance of their city as a welcome party for the incoming group. Tigun, Misarel and O'blame waited for them at the shipyard with other arrangements.

"Here they are," Misarel shouted as he saw them approaching through his *sifaar* (a telescope). "They are coming, Tigun."

Doperi soon reached White-ord with his group of men. Both Misarel and Tigun went up to him and hugged him in a happy reunion. "Don't...you'll crush my bones, I am not too strong," Doperi said as the two men hugged him tightly.

"You came, Doperi!" Misarel said excitedly.

"I could't say no to Sharptooth."

All of them, except O'blame, laughed.

"Nice work, Asto! You led them here and completed your first job perfectly well," Misarel complimented. "He is Tigun's son," Misarel told Doperi.

"Oh, good lord! Hello boy, how are you?!" Doperi asked.

"I am good, sir," Asto replied.

"So, will you be coming with us?"

"Yes."

Doperi looked at Tigun. "You both are brave," he said.

Almost fifty young lads had come with Doperi. "Listen, everyone," Misarel called out. "It's evening now. Please help yourself with tea, spicy crackers and sweet bread. It has been laid out for all of you. Tonight, we will drink and have dinner together. Enjoy, lads! We will party tonight. Take some rest now as you must be tired after the long journey, and have the refreshments. We will meet tonight."

The servants had been ordered to prepare a lavish dinner for that night. The place had been decorated with glazed papers, rolls and colourful banners. Small tents had been put up all across White-ord. Decorative candles hung everywhere with firelight. Doperi asked Tigun and Misarel, "What are we celebrating?"

O'blame interrupted, "Yes, I have been asking them the same thing. There was no need for all this."

"It is necessary. We are soon departing on a long and dangerous journey. This will motivate everyone to be loyal to us," Misarel explained.

"Quite good, Misarel," Doperi replied.

The celebration commenced as soon as it was night. A stage was set up where Misarel asked everyone to come and introduce themselves. Everyone did so one after the other–Bardi, Aaro Zinsha, Dun Lorezi, etc. Misarel started drinking gring and shouted to the others, "Take your grings, lads!" Everyone cheered and began drinking. Misarel then started singing the folk songs of Northly Earth. With a goblet of gring still in his hand, he began dancing too. Everybody clapped and cheered Misarel on. Tigun was sitting with Doperi and O' Blame in one corner.

Misarel came down from the stage and instructed everyone to dance. All the lads stood up and started dancing; some were singing too. Misarel grabbed Asto's hand and forced him repeatedly to dance too, but he refused every time. Everyone was having a great time. The whole shipyard had transformed into a party lawn where everyone was having the time of their lives, except for Doperi who had to listen to O'blame complain about the expenses of this celebration.

Misarel then asked Tigun to take the stage.

"Lads, did you all enjoy the night?" Tigun asked. All of them spoke 'Yes' in unison. "Now, eat your dinner and take rest for the night because we have to start the journey of our hunt tomorrow. Finish up your meals and proceed to your camps. Goodnight to all of you."

Post dinner, Tigun, Misarel and O'blame mutually decided to reach White-ord early the next morning.

CHAPTER 7

BEGINNING OF THE HUNT

Somedays ago, Tigun had told Asto's mother, Irita, that Asto would accompany him on this hunt due to Momunsha's bad health and inability to go with them. Irita hadn't agreed to it initially, but understood how necessary it was after sometime. She knew that this hunt was dangerous. The night before they were to leave, she sat beside Asto while he slept, and watched him the entire night.

In the morning, she said to him, "I have prepared sweet bread with butter, honey, some crackers and gullahony for you to take on your journey."

"There is no need for all this, Ma. We have plenty of food on the ship."

"It may be so, but I didn't make any of that. Take this," she insisted. Irita had packed some medicines and utensils for him as well. She reminded him over and over again to take them when needed.

The night before, Tigun and Holbaat had also told Momunsha about the hunt. He was upset since he couldn't be a part of this hunt, the biggest they had ever been on. Tigun and Holbaat made him understand, however, that he needed to stay back and get healed properly.

Tigun was prepared and ready to leave when Irita came up to him and pleaded, "Please, take care of Asto. He is just an innocent kid. He will not let you know even if he has some problem." She started crying. Tigun went near her and promised that he would protect Asto at any cost.

Momunsha called Asto to his room. When Asto entered, he found him standing, as if he had been waiting for him. "Remember Asto," he said, "You are the son of the brave Tigun. Never be afraid, always stay calm, and don't forget that you are from the Sword Runner's family."

Asto smiled at Momunsha and said, "Thanks, Momu."

Momunsha then gave him a beautifully crafted leather handled long knife. "Take this, Asto."

"But why, Momu? It's yours."

"Take it, kid. It will protect you, as it has protected me many times before."

"You know, Momu, I really love hunts. I always wished that I would go on my first hunt with you, not without." They hugged each other and came out into the outer garden where Tigun, Irita, Aziredun, Holbaat, Maliri (Holbaat's wife), and Valisha (Momunsha's wife) were waiting.

"Asto, come. We have to go," Tigun said.

Asto took everyone's blessings. Irita handed him a white stone attached to a golden chain. "This is our forefathers' sacred stone. It will help you. Believe in it and always wear it," she told Asto and tied it around his neck.

Tigun instructed Aziredun, his younger son, to take care of his mother and himself. Tigun and Asto now took everyone's leave. Irita was still sobbing. Azirdun ran up to Asto and hugged him. "Come back soon," he said to his brother with wet eyes.

Asto got tears in his eyes too. "Yes I will," he said.

Asto had worn a sky blue shirt and black skinny pants with boots. He also wore a brown half waistcoat on it. A long thin overcoat Tigun wore under which he wore brown shirt and black pants with brown boots.

Both father and son rode off to White-ord. They reached the shipyard to find Misarel talking to Doperi, while O'blame was sitting in one corner.

"Asto, you are late," Misarel said with a smile.

All the lads were looking fresh and ready for the hunt. Doperi and Tigun gathered them all near the ship and the latter started speaking, "We are ready to leave, men. It's a long journey. We have to take care of each other. I will take care of all of you, as I had promised to the mothers of Glosaang. You are all my brothers. At every situation, good or bad, you will find me near you."

"Sharptooth... Sharptooth... Sharptooth," all the lads started chanting together.

"Come on, my brothers. Promise me that you will never leave anyone alone. Be honest with your companions as I will always be with you."

O'blame asked, "Who is Sharptooth?" but nobody heard him.

"To Elt-duk!" Tigun yelled.

Misarel shouted loudly, "Hy hord!" *(Victory shall be ours!)*

"Hy hord!" All the others shouted after him and started boarding the ship.

Both Misarel and Tigun knew how to sail a ship, and in the past few days, Misarel had taught Asto a good deal about it too. From all the men who had come from Glosaang, Dun Lorezi and Aaro Zinsha knew how to sail. Both of them were called on deck. Misarel instructed them to pull off the big cloth that covered the name of the ship.

"What is the name of the ship, uncle Misarel?" Asto asked.

"See for yourself."

The cloth was removed by Dun and Aaro with the help of some other lads. It revealed the name 'DAFORT'.

"A big blue coloured ship with white outline. Great name!" Doperi said to Misarel. While Tigun and Misarel called upon Asto, Aaro Zinsha and Dun Lorezi to assist them in sailing, Doperi and O'blame tried to sharpen their vision with the sifaar.

Dafort was ready to set sail for the hunt to Elt-duk. The ship's horns blew loudly. Asto stood on the deck and innocently watched the coast of White-ord, remembering his mother and his bother with wet eyes. Taking their positions behind the oars, all the lads started singing victory songs, and they set sail.

This company of gold hunters was first headed towards a small island called 'Toop Of a Strey'. It was almost ten days of sailing away from Mirkota. "We can make it there in eight days, as our lads are strong and experienced," Misarel said.

Days on deck went by smoothly. Asto was still in training. He had improved greatly at swordplay besides map reading

and sailing. He talked to Doperi sometimes who told him about the various herbs and how they could be used on the human body.

After Toop Of a Strey, they were to head on a month long journey covering SIVAAN, then the LAKE CITY, BUK DIN DUK, and finally reach Elt-duk.

The island of Toop Of a Strey did not have many people residing on it, but the island was blessed with Nature's gifts. A special herb called *falus* grew there. It was useful to counter weakness, fever, and many another kinds of illnesses. It could be rubbed on or chewed. It showed results very quickly too. Not many people were aware of its availability, but Doperi knew about it. Yet, O'blame complained, "Why we are going there? It'll cost us extra."

Asto mingled well with the other lads. Dun Lorezi and Aaro Zinsha were both older than Asto. They talked about their village, their friends, and what all they had done in the past. Aaro Zinsha was the oldest of the three. He always asked Dun Lorezi and Asto to have gring with him, but they refused every time. "Life is short, do whatever you like," he always said. They often played card games in the cabin which they shared on the lower deck.

Almost seven days had passed since they started from Mirkota. Everybody now knew each other and treated each other like family.

"I think we will reach Toop Of a Strey the day after tomorrow," Tigun said. However, they reached there the very next day.

It was an old island that always remained in the shadows. Doperi had told Tigun and Misarel about this place when Tigun had gotten injured near Glosaang. He had healed

Tigun with *falus* then, which was why he had recovered so quickly. That had been the start of Doperi's friendship with Tigun and Misarel.

The island had a very small dock since no big ships ever stopped there, but Dafort was anchored there nonetheless. Everybody on board was happy to see land after a week's time.

Tigun and Doperi alighted the ship with Asto and some other men to gather falus in good quantity. They also bought some vegetables and fruits from the local market. Misarel and O'blame stayed on the ship for regular maintenance. They were scheduled to stay there for two days.

The party of men on land collected a good amount of falus from the forest and the local market. News spread on the island that a big group of hunters from Northly Earth had arrived. People thronged the coast to see the big ship. After two days, they set sail again, bidding a loud and cheerful farewell to the many people of Toop Of a Strey who had come to see them off.

The company of gold hunters continued their journey eastward towards Sivaan.

O'blame spent most of his time alone in his cabin, calculating expenses and potential incomes. Tigun and Misarel lived in a single huge cabin that had separate beds. All the planning and discussions usually took place in O'blame's cabin, or on the upper deck in the open.

Their latest discussion had been regarding their journey after Sivaan. It had been decided that after Sivaan, the company would set sail to the Lake City, but for that, they had to cross Rovanta, and the problem was Rovanta. Some time ago, Misarel and Tigun had gone hunting in Rovanta for a precious stone–*velum,* a green transparent stone which had remained undiscovered till Misarel and Tigun arrived in Rovanta with their hunters. They broke the rules of the town, fought with the guards and injured them. They stole the velum, which was worth 2000 Droshes. So, Tigun and Misarel were 'wanted' there. All the water-lines of Rovanta were checked by guards. A big ship like Dafort could not dodge the guards of Rovanta.

"You didn't tell me about this, Misarel," O'blame said in anger.

"This is not a big problem," Misarel said.

"Yes it is, you have cheated me. How can we cross Rovanta if you people are wanted there?" O'blame asked.

"We will cross Rovanta, Mr. O'blame. You should not worry," Misarel tried to pacify him, but he was in no mood to be satisfied.

"You always talk like that, Misarel. This time, it is serious."

"I am serious, Mr. O'blame. I am."

"Then tell me what the plan is?"

"We stole their velum. We broke the rules. We fought with the guards there. We have been declared criminals in Rovanta," Misarel started.

"That much I know," O'blame interrupted him.

"But the local lads joined us. We gave them more that their share because of the trust and loyalty that they showed in us. They will be ready to help us still. I am sure of it," Misarel explained.

“But how will they know that we are coming?” O’blame asked quickly.

Both Misarel and Tigun turned their gazes towards Ispichu who started cooing looking at both of them. “We will send Ispichu to them with a message. They will answer us,” said Tigun.

“What if Ispichu does not return? Or what if he does not reach there at all or gets lost on his way?” O’blame asked.

“Don’t underestimate him. He is quite smart and intelligent. He was with us when we went hunting in Rovanta. He knows where to go,” Tigun answered.

“He know the whole way to Elt-duk, Mr. O’blame,” Misarel said quietly. “Ispichu knows where our lads are in Rovanta. All we need to do is to tell him.“

“We will send Ispichu as soon as we reach Sivaan to inform our lads the time and date of our crossing Rovanta. They only have to give us some time to cross Rovanta’s waterlines,” Misarel explained the plan. Everybody was satisfied, except O’blame. His hand flew to his head. „Why did I come here with them?” he mumbled to himself.

Time to time, Misarel united everyone on the ship. They ate and drank together. Tigun and Misarel told them about their adventures and shared their experiences so that the men could prepare for the upcoming hunt. The wealth of Elt-duk was not going to be served to them on a plate; it was dangerous and full of surprises.

Tigun practiced swordplay with the lads and gave them tips for attack and defence. Doperi gave them advice on herbs from different places and how to use them.

One day, Asto was in Doperi's cabin. Doperi asked Asto, "Do you know, Asto, why your father wears a sharp tooth around his neck?"

"No," he replied.

Doperi then told him the story of Sharptooth and Tigun.

"He broke the tooth of that beast?"Asto asked excitedly.

"Yes, he did."

"Did he kill Sharptooth?"

"No, he didn't. But he beat Sharptooth in that battle."

Asto became excited when he heard the story, even more when he came to know that his father had defeat the giant beast. Asto continuously asked questions about Sharptooth. "How tall was Sharptooth? Where is he now?"

"He was very tall, Asto, three times the size of any man. It is said that he went back to Corga," Doperi answered. "Your father is a hero in Glosaang."

"Really?" Asto asked Doperi.

"Yes. And I know, Asto, Tigun never told you that story because he does not like to praise or talk about himself. He is a brave warrior and a great man. You know, Asto, what the people of Glosaang now call Tigun?"

"What?" Asto asked calmly.

"Sharptooth," Doperi replied.

"Sharptooth," Asto whispered to himself with his eyes wide, looking towards Doperi.

CHAPTER 8

Mysterious Island, Mysterious Man

Almost ten days after leaving Toop of a Strey, Tigun and Misarel started preparing Ispichu.

"We should finalise the date and time before crossing Rovanta," Tigun said.

"Yes, we will when we reach Sivaan. It is almost a four-day journey to Rovanta from there. We will tell the lads the exact day of crossing Rovanta," Misarel explained.

Asto was with Dun Lorezi and Aaro Zinsha at the time at the upper deck, making fun of O'blame, mimicking his voice and expressions. Suddenly, Misarel arrived and asked, "What are you doing, lads?"

"Nothing, sir,"Aaro Zinsha replied.

"Tell me, what are you doing?" he insisted.

"No...nothing, sir," he replied again while looking at Asto.

"I know you all are doing something. Tell me, I want to know too. I like laughing," Misarel now started having fun with them. "Are you making fun of Mr. O'blame?"

"No," all the three boys said in unison.

"If he comes to know that you are doing this, he will take this ship and go to Elt-duk alone and left us in deserted in Prancima river," Misarel said seriously, then laughed out loud. The banter continued. "Tell me, Asto. Who is your girlfriend?"

"No uncle, I don't have one," Asto replied shyly.

"You are lying. Isn't he lying?" Misarel asked Aaro Zinsha. He just smiled.

"Asto, you should have a girlfriend by now. Look, both of your other friends are married already," said Misarel. "Teach him something," he said to Dun Lorezi and Aaro Zinsha. Everyone smiled at each other. "Have fun, but also work hard. That's what I do," Misarel said to all of them. "I am going to having lunch now. You all should have your lunch too, then let's meet in the evening," said Misarel before going back to his cabin, while the rest of them resumed their work and fun again.

After lunch, Asto came to the upper deck, while Dun Lorezi and Aaro Zinsha stayed at their cabin. Tigun and Doperi were at the upper deck, talking about Glosaang and Northly Earth, which was not so flourishing like Southly Earth. Suddenly, Asto saw something from his sifaar. He took it off his sight and cleared its with his wool jacket, then looked thought it again. The sight made him scream, "Pa... Pa, come here fast. Look! Flying beasts!"

"What are you saying? Are you mad? There is no such thing as a flying beast," Tigun replied. "Give me the sifaar," he commanded, taking the sifaar from his son.

"I have never heard of such a thing," said Doperi.

Tigun tried to focus through the sifaar, and remained silent for almost five to ten seconds. Asto and Doperi both kept looking at Tigun, expecting him to say something. “What are they?” Tigun asked himself. Doperi snatched the sifaar from Tigun and looked through it, but the sight made him turn to stone.

“Uncle Doperi, what do you see? Pa, what is it? Who are they?”

Listening to all this commotion, Misarel and O’blame arrived at the scene too. “What happened?” Misarel asked.

“There is a flying beast there,”Asto replied.

“What? There is no such thing as a flying beast. Give me the sifaar.”

Tigun called Aaro Zinsha and instructed him to bring more sifaars for everybody to see what Asto had said.

They were big brown creatures with a creepy face, sharp teeth, big ears, structured almost like a man with small legs. Instead of hands, however, they had wide spanned wings with sharp nails at the end, and a tail.

“What are they?” Misarel wondered aloud. “Good lord! We have seen many different kinds of beasts on our adventures, but these are amazing!”

“How many are there?” O’blame asked.

“Three,” Doperi replied.

“But what are they doing here and what land is that?” Tigun asked.

“I don’t know,” Misarel replied. “Aaro, bring the big map here, and Tigun, start finding the location of this land.”

The big map was placed on the table and everyone crouched over it, calculating their own position on it. The map didn't show any land or island near them. The only pieces of land between Toop Of a Strey and Sivaan were some small islands of Sivaan, but even the nearest one was about three days of sailing away from their current location. This land had not been charted by the cartographers. Nobody knew about this island that they were looking at from Dafort. They left the map and took to their sifaars again as they approached the island.

"They are fighting with someone," Tigun said.

"How do you know?" Doperi asked.

"They are flying upwards then coming down again. There is someone there behind the trees with whom they are fighting," Tigun explained. "Oh, did you hear that?" Tigun said surprisedly.

"What?" Misarel asked.

"They are also screaming."

"They are fighting a man, Pa," Asto said.

"A man!? A man can't fight with them."

"Yes, he is a man," Misarel replied.

"A man, fighting with these beasts? But why are they fighting?" everyone asked one another.

"Turn the ship! Don't go any closer to them," O'blame said. "It will be too dangerous for us."

Dun Lorezi took the wheel and started turning the ship hard right.

"Wait," Tigun yelled. "I think we should go and save that man. Maybe he needs us, he is alone."

"What? What are you saying? Why should we care if he is alone or not?" O'blame replied.

"He is fighting with those flying beasts, and he is a human. It is our duty to help him as a human being. Do we just stay and watch him die in front of us?" Tigun asked.

"That's why I want to turn the ship," O'blame answered. "Dun Lorezi, turn the ship!" O'blame ordered again.

"Asto, bring my bow and arrows," Tigun commanded.

"What? Are you a fool? They will attack us too," O'blame said in a frightened manner.

"I don't care. I will save that man," Tigun replied in anger.

"But why, Tigun? Why?" Misarel interposed.

"What are you saying, Misarel? We should save him," Tigun replied.

"O'blame is right, Tigun. We have to leave from here. We still have a long journey ahead of us. We can't take such a risk now."

"How can you talk like that, Misarel? We are humans, we have saved so many lives before. Have you forgotten, Misarel?"

"No, I haven't, Tigun. But right now, it is a different situation. We don't know anything about those beasts, or how many they are. We can't put everybody's life on stake to save just one man," Misarel tried to calm Tigun down.

Doperi had been watching the whole scene from his sifaar. "They are leaving," Doperi said. "They are leaving now," he repeated more loudly. "And I think he has killed one of the beasts and has hurt another. The two are now taking the dead one away with them."

Tigun and Misarel started watching through the sifaar again.

"Yes, they are going, they are going south," Doperi continued. "The man is screaming. I can cure him," Doperi spoke slowly. Tigun glared at Misarel.

"What?" Misarel asked. "Fine. Dun Lorezi, go straight ahead," Misarel ordered.

"What are you saying Misarel?" O'blame said angrily. "You can't do this. It is non of our business," O'blame went on protesting, but Dun Lorezi took the straight way towards the mysterious island and the mysterious man.

After a while, Dafort touched the land of the unknown island. Tigun gathered everyone, except O'blame, with swords, shields, bows and arrows. "Misarel, cover the sky," Tigun commanded. They started searching the small forest for the man.

Suddenly, Doperi said, "Blood! Maybe it's his blood." They followed the blood trail into the forrest.

Asto screamed, "Pa! I found him."

"Where?"

"He is behind that bush."

"Asto, get behind me," Tigun commanded.

As Tigun approached the man, he attacked Tigun, but he took him on his body and both of them fell down. Tigun removed him from over himself. The man had become unconscious. Doperi checked him.

"Take him to the ship. We should not stay here for long," Tigun said. Everyone started marching towards the ship, taking the man on a wooden stretcher.

The man looked quite older in age with long white hair and a beard, but had a tall and strong built. He was wearing a full-length white *dhoti* around his waist and had another white cloth that went over his left shoulder and tucked into the right side of his waist. He had an axe in one hand and a bow over his other shoulder. There were no arrows in his quiver. Doperi gave him some quetish and falus together. "I have to clean his wounds. I will take care of him, don't worry," he said.

O'blame was simply angry with the action that the company had taken. "I shouldn't have come here," he muttered to himself.

"What now?" Misarel asked.

"We will cure him. When he is healed, we will leave him at one of our stoppages," Tigun answered.

"And what about those creatures we saw?" Misarel asked again.

"We shall ask him about those," Tigun replied.

What we saw today was indeed something quite weird, so different and horrible," Misarel spoke in a curious manner.

"Yes," Tigun answered. "Let's rest now."

"Yes," Misarel replied.

They went back to their cabin with many questions in their minds about those creatures and the elderly man whom they had rescued and was now resting in their ship. It was a long night through which the answers of many questions were desired, but nobody knew what was hidden within the womb of the Earth.

The next morning, Tigun, Misarel, and O'blame gathered on the upper deck. Dafort was now sailing towards Sivaan as per schedule. O'blame started the conversation, "Why are we wasting our herbs on him? We don't know how many more days he will take to heal!"

"Maybe one week, or maybe a month," Misarel replied.

"What?" O'blame almost screamed.

"His wounds are deep, and he is an old man. We will leave him at our next stoppage," Tigun cleared the situation.

At that moment, Doperi came up to them hurriedly and exclaimed, "He is awake."

"What? So fast!" Misarel said surprisedly.

"He muttered in his sleep the entire night. He also took the name of Elt-duk, Buk din duk, and the Als–mites," Doperi told them.

"Als-mites, God's men?" Misarel asked with surprise.

"Yes," Doperi said. "I don't think he is a normal man. No one can recover so quickly after receiving such wounds and broken bones, that too at this age," Doperi replied.

"Can we meet him?" Tigun asked.

"You don't need to come to me."

Everyone turned their heads in the direction of the voice to see the tall man standing in front of them. Everyone stood up to see him. Asto, Aaro Zinsha and Dun Lorezi also came to see him.

"Are you alright Mr…?" Tigun started.

"Buk Parsomin. My name is Buk Parsomin and I am quite good now. Thanks for the treatment, Mr…?"

"Tigun, Tigun Sword Runner."

"And Mr..." Buk Parsomin turned to Doperi.

"Doperi Thilmus."

"Where have you come from?" Tigun asked him.

"I am from Buk din duk," he replied.

"Oh, so you are a saint," Misarel interrupted.

"I am a warrior saint," he replied. "You know about Buk din duk?"

"Yes, we know," Misarel replied. "But who were those creatures with whom you were fighting on that island?" he asked.

He ignored Misarel's question and asked, "Where are you people heading?"

"We are going nowhere," Misarel answered angrily.

"To Elt-duk?" he asked.

"Who told you?" Misarel asked.

"You said it yourself and very loudly. I heard it, Mr...?"

"Misarel Wiser is my name."

"Okay, Mr. Misarel. We need to turn this ship right now," Parsomin said aloud.

O'blame stepped forward hurriedly and said, "Are you mad? We are going straight to Sivaan, then Lake city, then Elt-duk. Who are you to order us? Get off my ship right now."

"So it is true that you are going to Elt-duk. Are you fools? Do you want to get yourself killed?" Parsomin said in anger.

"What are you talking about?" Tigun asked.

"I am talking about Elt-duk which is not safe for anyone," Parsomin replied.

"We know Elt-duk is not safe, but we are experienced in hunting in forests and mountains. We are not amateurs," Misarel said.

Parsomin looked at Asto and said, "Indeed." After a pause, he continued, "I understand, you people are going for the gold & wealth of Elt-duk."

"It's none of your business, Mr. Parsomin," Tigun replied, "We are on our own and we know what we are doing. You should take rest. We will leave you at Sivaan, then you can continue your journey any which way."

Buk Parsomin became silent for a while. "Mr. Misarel, you wanted to know who I was fighting back the island? They are the Burburuks."

"What are they?" Misarel asked curiously.

"When you get to Elt-duk, you will find many Burburuks and Trroths there."

"What rubbish! Trroths are a myth, they were lost centuries ago," Misarel replied. "Look, we are gold hunters. We have been doing this from many years in Other Lands, Rovanta, Falini and many more."

"Oh, so you are an expert company of thieves?" Parsomin said.

"We are not thieves," Tigun replied angrily. "We only hunt for unclaimed wealth and help the poor with it, of course after taking our share from it."

Parsomin walked down to the edge of the ship, then turned around and said, "Burburuks are ancient creatures who can fly and sometimes run. The bad news is that the Trroths have made them their pets. All the burburuks now do what the Trroths want. Trroths want Elt-duk and Elt-duk wants its ruler," he explained.

"Why are you talking about these things? It is not the first age of men on Earth," Misarel said with a fury rising in him.

"We should turn the ship around and head west towards the kingdom of Monaar where we might find some help," Parsomin continued.

"I think he has gone mad. Those wounds were deep," Misarel said.

"The entire Southly Earth is in danger. The Trroths want to take revenge on men because King Volesalt, son of the great king Ballanduall, betrayed the Trroth King and killed him. Trroths now want to occupy Elt-duk to become unbeatable. Men are not capable of fighting with them on their own. Als-mites are not so strong anymore to fight with the Trroths again, as they did before, and if Southly Earth is captured, Northly Earth will be next. They will not leave a single human alive on this Earth. Death will spread everywhere soon," Parsomin explained.

Everybody listened to him, but without trust.

You should rest," Tigun finally said.

"What rest? He is a fool. Get him off the ship right now," O'blame said and advanced towards Parsomin. Parsomin raised his hand and motioned to push against him without making contact. O'blame flew backwards and fell far away. Everybody got surprised by that incident.

'Don't come any closer to me. This is my first and last warning," Parsomin warned.

"Do you think that will scare us?" Misarel questioned.

"I don't want you to be afraid, but you should not head towards where you've planned, because only death is waiting for you there."

"Why should we believe in you?" Misarel asked.

"How did you come to know about the wealth of Elt-duk?" Parsomin asked.

"When we were at Rovanta, I met a saint. He told me about the blaze of Elt-duk. He was from Buk din duk. He gave me this piece of gold from the blaze," Misarel said and showed Parsomin the coin from his pocket.

Looking at the coin from both sides, Parsomin said, "Yes, it is from Elt-duk. The face in this coin is of the great King Ballanduall."

"You know the face?" Tigun asked curiously.

"Yes," Parsomin replied.

Misarel took the coin back from Parsomin and said, "I sent Ispichu, our trained pigeon, to Elt-duk to gather information about the mountain and the blaze. When he returned, he told us everything about the route and the wealth he saw there, the shining gold and the gems."

"How did he tell you?" Parsomin asked.

"My friend Tigun and I can understand Ispichu's language," Misarel said with pride.

"So you have something special. Very nice," Parsomin said. "May I see that pigeon?"

"Asto, bring Ispichu here," Misarel ordered.

"Who's son is he?" Parsomin asked about Asto.

"He is my son," Tigun replied.

"What's his name?"

"Asto, Asto Sword Runner is my name," Asto replied before disappearing down the deck. After a while, he came back up with Ispichu.

"Very nice," Parsomin whistled upon seeing Ispichu. Ispichu stared at Parsomin, a new face. "Hello, Mr. Ispichu. Many things rely on you now. Tell me the truth."

"How will he tell you anything?" Misarel asked Parsomin.

"Let's see," Parsomin answered.

CHAPTER 9

ISPICHU'S TALE

Parsomin sat down on the floor and made Ispichu perch on his right hand. Misarel wondered why Ispichu was not flying away, since Parsomin was unknown to Ispichu. Parsomin started chanting with his eyes closed, "*Bilshore Ameto No Phikon Walari.*"[4]

After a moment, Ispichu closed his eyes too and sat down. Everyone on the deck was confused about what was going on in front of them, and they started asking questions from each other. After some moments, Parsomin started speaking, "I was happy when Misarel choose me to go to Elt-duk to gather information about the blaze of Elt-duk. I love Tigun and Misarel, they brought me up. I decided to fly speedily to Elt-duk." While listening to this from Buk Parsomin, it seemed as if Parsomin had entered Ispichu, or perhaps Ispichu had entered Buk Parsomin.

"I took the route of Valdus and reached there in almost a day. I took rest in Araborn's tree nest. The next day, I ate some wheat grains and started my journey towards Sivaan. It is a beautiful place, an island surrounded by water. I had reached Sivaan in almost five days. Rovanta was my

4 Magical chants come from the language of Alsami, the language of the Als-mites. Both the names 'Elt-duk' and 'Buk din duk' came from the Alsami language.

next stop. It is a horrible place. I remember, we had barely escaped from there some time ago. Their guards had almost captured us. They had wanted to kill us because of the Velum stone that we stole from their town, but the local lads of Rovanta had helped us escape. I went to Barshaw's house and gave him Misarel's message. After reading the message, Barshaw gave me a cabin and some food. I rested there for three days, then started my journey again.

"I took my leave from Barshaw and Rovanta with happiness. I started quickly so I could reach the Lake City soon, but for that, I had to cross the Bloon river. Winds were stronger over the Bloon river. I could hardly keep good speed. When the heavy rain started, I took shelter in a tree on the edge of the river. I planned to stay there over night. Some other birds were there too, talking about strange things in a dark forest and Buk din duk. A raven was talking about strange folks passing through Elt-duk. A bat described the presence of strange big birds. I didn't pay any attention towards them. They asked me about myself and my journey, but I didn't tell them much. The next morning, I flew to Lake City. The sun was shining and I calculated that I would reach the Lake City by nightfall. I reached Lake City and found my friend's nest where I had planned to stay the night. It was in a Cuesbuk tree at the white garden center of the castle. I love Lake City as there are many gardens, fountains and ponds there. My friend welcomed me into his nest. We talked much through the night and slept very little. The next morning, we went to the main garden of the castle where the Queen fed the pigeons. We ate a lot there and took rounds of the castle. After that, we visited the many different gardens of the city–blue garden, yellow garden, red garden. I saw very lovely scenes there."

At the ship, everybody's jaw dropped to the ground in shock. They could not believe what was going on in front of them.

"I thanked my friend and left for Elt-duk," Parsomin continued. "My friend told me the route to Elt-duk as he had once lived there. When I reached Buk din duk, I saw big birds flying below me. I had never seen birds so big as them before. I was frightened, so I hid myself in a tree. Those birds vanished in the morning, but were replaced by many people there. As opposed to the horrible night before, they looked fine to me. I resolved to keep flying towards Elt-duk.

"My friend had warned me that Elt-duk was not easy to fly to. One had to cross river Horrifa, which was dangerous. One always has to keep one's eyes open because a fish beast lives in that river. It can catch any bird from any height. It is one of the most dangerous creatures living in river Horrifa. When I reached Horrifa, I made a plan. I stayed at the river side for three days and studied at what times the beast jumped out of the water to catch the birds, and how high it could jump. On the 4th day, I decided to cross river Horrifa. The fish beast didn't see me, as it had caught a bird only the previous day and was not hungry. I crossed Horrifa unscathed.

"Elt-duk was in front of me, so I start flying faster. I saw the great mountain, long and wide, ice-covered on the top. I perched on a rock and saw Elt-duk which seemed to touch the sky itself. I started to fly towards it in search of the glowing stones, gems and gold. I didn't see any glowing stones the entire way. But when I searched for the same at night, I found the glowing stones, many glowing stones, and gems there. I was very happy. Wherever I looked, I saw glowing things.

I wanted to tell everything to Misarel as soon as possible, but I suddenly heard someone screaming. It was the same big bird that I had seen at Buk din duk. There were more of those big birds here, screaming, maybe talking to each other. I couldn't understand what they were and what they were doing. I flew away from there and took a round high up in the sky, circling Elt-duk, and noted the places where the stones were glowing so that I may guide Misarel to them later. I saw that those big birds were with humans. Then, I took leave from Elt-duk. I was happy that I had good news to give to Misarel. I was missing Tigun, Misarel, and Mirkota, so I flew back home."

Silence presided over the upper deck of Dafort for some time. Ispichu opened his eyes and flew towards Tigun. The connection between Ispichu and Parsomin had ended. Parsomin opened his eyes and stood up.

"Now you understand," Parsomin said and fainted.

"What happened to him?" Tigun asked.

"Perhaps he consumed all his energy in connecting with Ispichu, since he was not fully healed from his fight with the flying beasts," Doperi explained. Aaro Zinsha and Dun Lorezi carried Parsomin back to his cabin. Tigun, Misarel, Doperi, and O'blame seated themselves in chairs and tried to understand what had just happened.

"He knows magic," Misarel said.

"Yes," Tigun replied.

"What do you think about what you just heard, Misarel?" Tigun asked.

"Maybe it's true," Misarel replied while looking at Doperi.

"Listen lads, both of you know what Ispichu said to you and only you know whether what Parsomin said is true or false," Doperi cleared the confusion.

"Hmm," both Tigun and Misarel replied.

"Parsomin cooked up a fake story because he wants to go to Monaar and prevent us from going to Elt-duk, but the ship will not turn. We will head straight to Elt-duk and claim our wealth," O'blame said exasperatedly.

"That decision lies with both of them, Mr. O'blame," Doperi interposed. "Only they know whether what Ispichu told them and what he told Buk Parsomin is the same thing or not. If it is not the same, we should leave Mr. Buk Parsomin at Sivaan, but if it was the same, then we are in big trouble, Mr. O'blame. Our lives are far more important than any amount of wealth, if the scenario is indeed as Mr. Buk Parsomin says," Doperi explained to Mr. O'blame. Both Doperi Thilmus and O'blame looked at Tigun and Misarel.

Tigun asked Misarel, "Did Ispichu tell you about the Burburuks?"

"No, he only mentioned the big birds. I thought he saw Garuds, as they come to Buk din duk sometimes," Misarel replied.

"What about the humans he mentioned?" Doperi asked.

"Yes, Ispichu had mentioned the humans, that is why I had been so eager to go to Elt-duk as early as possible for a hunt," replied Misarel. Everyone became numb for a while.

As Tigun and Misarel's conversation took the same track as Buk Parsomin's, O'blame got depressed. He understood that Parsomin was right. The wealth of Elt-duk was looking like an impossible dream now. He held his head in his hands and mumbled, “I shouldn’t have come here.”

At night, everyone returned to their cabins, but nobody could sleep. The day had been quite heavy for everyone. Everything had changed now, their plans, their preparation, their schedule, their expenses for the hunt–everything now seemed to be in vain. All the effort that the company had made was laid waste. Many hopes had relied on this hunt. Many lives were dependant upon this hunt and its wealth. Everyone was thinking about the hunt and the situation which had now arisen before them. Elt-duk was more dangerous now, and the company knew this. To continue their journey to Elt-duk was to play with their own lives.

Some action had to be taken the next day which would give direction to their journey.

CHAPTER 10

A Saint's Story

The next morning, Tigun, Misarel, Doperi, and O'blame gathered on the deck for breakfast. They sat down on chairs, while the breakfast was served to them by a servant. They started talking about the incidents of the day before. Dafort was anchored until they arrived upon a decision. They heard Parsomin arriving with Asto and Aaro Zinsha.

"Why are you bringing him here, Asto?" Misarel shouted.

"I urged him to take me," Parsomin replied.

"You can barely walk," Misarel said to Parsomin.

"I know, but it was necessary for me to come here," Parsomin replied. Asto and Aaro Zinsha helped him sit in a chair.

"Bardi, give some tea and sweet bread to Mr. Parsomin," Tigun ordered. Bardi was a sweet-tempered boy who was also the ship's cook.

"Just tea. Thank you," Parsomin replied.

"Why don't you take rest, Mr. Parsomin?" Tigun asked while siping his tea.

"You are not aware of the things that are going to happen in the near future, Mr. Tigun. This is the last chance that God has given me to continue what we people started."

Bardi served hot tea with some sweet bread to Parsomin.

"What did you start? And what do you mean by 'we people'?" Misarel asked. Asto and Aaro Zinsha took their tea from Bardi and stood next to Parsomin.

"I told you, I am a warrior saint. We are aware of the recent actions of the Trroths. They are trying to return to power and have made the Burburuks their pets. We alone don't have the strength to march to Elt-duk and fight them. My chief, Din Erabel, and I are gathering warrior saints. I was ordered to go look for the Als-mites to ask for their help, so I had prepared to march to the dark forest with some of my fellow warrior saints."

"It is said that the Als-mites live far away from all the other lands and can't be seen by anyone," Tigun said.

Parsomin smiled as he took a sip of his tea. "Yes, you are right. But there is a secret place in the dark forest that leads to Corga in a minute," he replied. Everyone listened to him calmly.

"Is that true?" Asto asked Parsomin.

"Yes, Asto. It's true."

"How did you reach this mysterious island? Nobody knows about that island and it is not even marked on any of the maps," Misarel asked.

"I was trying to reach the dark forest with the other saints when there was a sudden attack on us by the Burburuks. They killed many saints and took the others with them. I don't know where most of them went, but I was taken to the island where you found me. That island has been created out of bad magic of the ancient evil. They wanted to eat me. I fought with them. When they thought that I was dead, they came near me, but I killed one of them. They flew away with the dead one. I wondered how I would escape from the island and reach the Als-mites? That's when you people came to me like a new ray of the Sun."

"Thank Tigun. He fought with everyone here to save you," Doperi said.

"There is no need for that, Doperi," Tigun replied.

"I am glad, Tigun Sword Runner, and thank you, Mr. Doperi. Your herbs healed me quite quickly," Parsomin expressed his feelings.

"So, it's true that the Trroths are back with the Burburuks under them, and Elt-duk has now been captured by them? But who are the humans with them that Ispichu mentioned?" Misarel asked eagerly.

"Those, my friend, are the Trroths themselves. Ispichu didn't see them clearly, only their man-like structure. Ispichu's vision clearly reveals that the Trroths have now started taking over Elt-duk," Parsomin explained.

"Why is Elt-duk spewing out gold and precious stones?" Tigun asked.

"When the ruler of Elt-duk is near, the mountain welcomes him in this way," Parsomin replied.

"We have to take some decision then," Misarel said. "If we do not go to Elt-duk, where do we go?"

"We should go to the kingdom of Monaar. We can seek help and make strategy with the King there," Parsomin said.

"But why should *we* go to Monaar? If we are not going to Elt-duk, we should return home," Misarel said.

"What rubbish! The whole of humanity is in danger, and you want to go back home?" Parsomin asked.

"The danger is in Southly Earth. Why should we concern ourselves with it?" Misarel asked.

"Yes, of course. We don't have to concern ourselves with the Trroths or the matters of Southly Earth," O'blame jumped into the conversation.

"Will it be of your concern when Southly Earth is completely captured by the Trroths? Do you think that they will not come to claim Northly Earth too after winning over Southly Earth?" Parsomin asked, then continued, "Northly Earth is weak, leaderless and scattered as it is. It won't require them much effort to snatch it for themselves. If we do not alert the kingdoms of men in the south about the Trroths and their dangerous quest, there is no chance for any kingdom to survive in the long run. If we alert them now and fight against them united and with full strength, there is a chance of survival.

"You think it wrong to concern yourselves with the matters of Southly Earth, but I feel it is the only bet we have for our survival as a whole. Who can decide what the right thing is and what wrong? Southly Earth doesn't matter to you because you do not live there, but what if you did live there? My concerns are not divided by kingdoms and geography. The whole Earth is my mother which has been feeding me for many years. If the Trroths had been trying to capture Northly Earth before Southly Earth, you would have found me begging every kingdom and the Als-mites to help Northly Earth, and then at the front line of battle against the Trroths," Parsomin explained in anger and everybody became silent.

"It is your wish, whichever way you want to go. This is your last chance, however. You can either help unite all goodness and positivity in this world against cruelty and madness, or you can go home and wait for things to end, which will surely not end in the way you wish. They will kill every man, woman and child, or make them all their slaves. Do you people want to get killed without a fight?" Parsomin asked.

"What difference does it make if we are from Northly Earth or Southly Earth? If the Trroths had attacked Northly Earth, wouldn't we have expected the same help from Southly Earth?" Tigun joined the conversation. "This may be our chance, perhaps Parsomin is right," he supported Buk Parsomin and turned towards Doperi who also nodded his head in support. Everybody remained silent for a while.

Suddenly, O'blame said, "Give me my money back, Misarel. I trusted you. You gave me your word that we would earn good money."

"I am in trouble too, Mr. O'blame. Tigun and I have spent a good amount of our money too, and we have worked hard for this hunt."

"Keep calm, Mr. O'blame," Doperi tried to pacify him.

"We should return home," O'blame said, then immediately corrected himself, "No, I have many debts there. We can't go back to Mirkota. Misarel, we should go somewhere else for hunting. You must know many places with unclaimed gold." He flitted between Tigun and Misarel, continuously blubbering loudly, "You must know many places for hunting, Tigun. We should go somewhere else. Tell me the place!"

Buk Parsomin was listening to everything. He shouted suddenly, "Keep quiet! I think I will have to do something harsh now." He started chanting again, "*Aldore omagum virgil vatama.*"

Everyone watched him curiously as to what he would do next. In a second, Parsomin split himself into two, three, four, five different versions of himself. The rest of them couldn't believe their eyes. One of the Parsomins went to haul up Dafort's anchor, while the other handled the wheel. Parsomin shouted, "Oarsmen, grab your oars! We have to sail west."

All the lads in the lowest deck started paddling speedily. It seemed as if they had come under the control of Parsomin's voice. Misarel stepped ahead to grab the wheel, but another Parsomin stopped him. Tigun came to free Misarel, but another Parsomin blocked Tigun.

"Do you want to fight us?" Tigun asked.

"No, I want you all to unite with us," Parsomin replied. Both Misarel and Tigun stood calmly. O'blame didn't try to do anything, as he was too scared after his previous attempt.

Buk Parsomin, the one who was at the ship's wheel started to turn the ship. The anchor had now been pulled up. Suddenly, Parsomin shut his eyes and whispered something. All the other Parsomins vanished. "If you still don't want to go, it's okay," he said and fell down unconscious.

Asto checked his pulse and said, "He has fainted again. I told him not to leave his bed this morning, that nobody would understand what he wished to do, but Mr. Parsomin told me, '*I feel goodness and positivity in your father, Asto. He will understand me. I have to show something to Misarel, after which he will understand me too. I must go, Asto. Our earth is in danger. Our lands, our houses, our generations are in danger. There are people who are still unaware of the danger, innocent people and kids. They will all be killed by the Trroths. The Trroths want to take revenge on men. They got betrayed by King Volesalt in the past. I will have to fight. Otherwise, what will we have to give to our children? What will we have to give to you, Asto? Slavery? Death? No, never. You and the other children are our future, Asto. We have to save our future.*' Isn't it of worth then to fight?"

Everybody remained quite and calm. Dun Lorezi came with a stretcher, and Asto, Aaro Zinsha and Dun Lorezi took Parsomin back to their cabin.

CHAPTER 11

The Turning Point

Dafort was now unanchored and had turned westward.

Tigun looked at Doperi and then at Misarel. With a straight face, he said, “I think this was all in our fate. We headed out to capture the unclaimed wealth of Elt-duk, but it seems that we will have to save it from the devil first. We have claimed Earth’s precious gifts for our survival many times before, but now it’s time to repay her debt. It is our fate. I know we are not prepared for this, but this is the truth. We are in danger, but someone has to take a decision. I have a young son with me. I was afraid for him even when we had left with only the hunt of Elt-duk in our minds because he is not experienced and Elt-duk has always been dangerous, but the situation has become even more dangerous now. What should I do then? Still, I don’t think going back is the answer. You all know the fable of the fire in the forest. While all the animals were running away, a small bird put out the fire by transferring water from a river in her small beak. When a passing owl asked her why she was doing that, and how she could possibly put out the huge fire with the water in her small beak, she replied, ‘Maybe I won’t be able to put out the fire with my little beak, but in history, I will be known not among those who set the fire or ran from it, but those who tried to put it out.' Right now, we are like those animals of the forest. What do we want to become, those who run away, or like the bird who tried her best to save the forest? The choice is ours!"

Bardi, the cook, came forward and said, "To the Earth, sir!"

Doperi looked at Bardi, then looked at Tigun. "To the Earth, Tigun!" he shouted.

"To the Earth!" Doperi and Bardi start shouting together. Tigun joined them too and they looked expectantly at Misarel. Misarel said nothing. All three of them stopped shouting. Misarel stepped forward towards them and said loudly, "To the Earth!"

Tigun drew out his sword and flourished it in the air. The chant 'To the Earth!' echoed all across the deck. Only O'blame sat alone in a corner wondering why he had come with them. The hunt which had started for Earth's precious gems and metals had now transformed into a mission to save the Earth.

Bardi excitedly told the news to Asto, Aaro Zinsha and Dun Lorezi.

"Is it true?" asked Asto.

"Yes, Asto, it is true. I am going to tell everyone about the decision."

Asto was happy to hear it. He wanted to convey this to Parsomin, but he was still unconscious. Aaro Zinsha asked how Mr. O'blame had agreed to this decision. "Surely he said, *I shouldn't have come here*," he mimicked him and they all started laughing.

Preparations were now being made to go to Monaar. Tigun and Misarel studied the maps closely.

"Monaar is far away from here," Misarel said.

"Yes, it is almost double of what we have completed already," Tigun replied.

"We will have to sail in good speed," Misarel said.

"Our lads are strong, we will encourage them," Doperi replied.

The next day, Asto came to the upper deck where everyone was having tea.

"How's Parsomin?" Tigun asked him.

"Still sleeping,"Asto replied.

"I think he might just come up in a few minutes," Misarel mocked Parsomin.

"Yes, every time he faints, he marches right back to us the next morning," Tigun joined in the mockery too and everyone started laughing.

Dafort continued its sail towards Monaar for the next two days, but Parsomin didn't wake up.

"How is he now?" Tigun asked Doperi, while they stood outside Parsomin's cabin. "Still unconscious. I think he knows that we are now going to Monaar. That's why he is not waking up," Doperi replied.

"His aim is bigger than our thoughts. Take care of him, Doperi."

"I will," Doperi answered.

The next afternoon, they were all sitting together after lunch, discussing the problems that were occurring in

Southly Earth, when Misarel said, "Maybe we will face the demons after some time."

"Yes, of course," came a voice from a distance. Everyone turned their head towards its direction.

"So, you're awake!" Tigun said.

"Will you faint again after showing us some magic?" Misarel asked, making everybody laugh. Parsomin laughed too.

"No, not anymore. I am healed properly, thanks to Mr. Doperi and of course Asto. They took very good care of me."

"Why did you always faint after performing some magic?" Misarel asked.

"Performing magic takes a lot of my energy, you see. To make you understand the point of going to Monaar was tough, and it cost me a lot of energy. Plus, I was weak and the magic drew out too much energy from my already injured body," Parsomin replied.

"What was that magic where you split into many?" Misarel asked.

"*Suvatma*," Parsomin replied.

"How do you do that?"

"I am a saint of Buk din duk, and I am Buk Parsomin, so I can do that," he replied.

"Bardi, give some food to Parsomin," Tigun shouted.

"Misarel, you raised a point about facing the Trroths in the near future," Parsomin said. "Why don't we prepare for that?"

"Prepare for what exactly?" Misarel asked.

"For war," Parsomin replied. "I don't want to ruin the pleasant atmosphere here, but we have to understand the seriousness of this situation. We should prepare for the upcoming events."

While Parsomin was saying this, Tigun turned to look at Asto and his innocent face, thinking that he had made a big mistake by bringing Asto along, especially since this hunt had now become so much more dangerous.

"What do you say, Tigun?" Parsomin asked. Tigun didn't reply, as he was still thinking deeply about Asto and his mistake of having brought him along. "Tigun!" Parsomin called again.

"Yes, yes?" he said, as if pulled suddenly out of deep thought.

"Are you thinking something?" Parsomin asked.

"Nothing," Tigun replied. Parsomin smiled.

"Do you think we can start trained ourselves?" Parsomin asked again.

"Yes, yes, we can start. It will be good for us," Tigun answered. "Let's start today."

It was decided that Parsomin, Tigun and Misarel would teach the whole crew how to defend themselves and fight, both with and without a weapon. That evening, Tigun arrived early at the upper deck where the training was to take place. Parsomin arrived soon after too.

"Mr. Tigun," he greeted. "You arrived early."

"Oh yes, you too," Tigun replied.

"I know, Mr. Tigun, that you are worried about Asto," Parsomin said.

"No, it's nothing like that," Tigun replied.

"I know that when I was talking about war, you were continuously watching him. I know you feel bad for having brought him here too," he said.

"I don't want to take him there, Mr. Parsomin. My elder brother's son, Momunsha, is usually always the one who accompanies us on our hunts. But he was injured and unable to come with us to Elt-duk. I had always thought that Asto has no interest in our hunts, but I recently got to know that he knows about each one of them. In the absence of Momunsha, Misarel also wanted that Asto should come with us. Asto got ready to join us too, since he was doing nothing before it. We knew Elt-duk is dangerous, and I promised Asto's mother that I would take care of him in any situation and at any cost. But the situation now is very different and far more dangerous. I know I have taken a decision which is almost suicidal," Tigun explained.

"I can understand, Mr. Tigun. You are a big hearted and generous man, and so is your son. Both of you think about the good of people, without even knowing them personally. You fought for me without knowing who I was. Anything could have happened on that island. Likewise, your son took care of me without knowing who I was. I could have been either good or bad, but what your son and you have shown me is what we call purity, Mr. Tigun. Your son will grow up to be a kind man. The future needs him. Mr. Tigun, you don't need to worry about Asto. The future will take care of him," Parsomin said.

Tigun didn't understand much about his reference to the future, but he said thanks. As soon as Tigun began to walk away, Parsomin held his hand. Tigun turned his head towards him and saw that his eyes were turned upwards and he was murmuring something.

"NORTHLY EARTH IS SCATTERED, THE REALM OF PRANCE WILL END, A LEADER WILL BE BORN, MEN WILL UNITE WHEN KINDNESS WILL SPREAD AGAIN, THE TEST HAS STARTED, EVERYONE NEEDS TO PROVE, KEEP FAITH IN YOURSELVES AND THE GOODNESS WHICH EXISTS IN THIS WORLD."

After saying this, Parsomin left Tigun's hand. "What did you say?" Tigun asked.

"A message." Saying this, Parsomin left.

After sometime, all the men arrived on the deck where the drills and preparations were to begin. Tigun, Misarel, Parsomin, Doperi, Asto, Aaro Zinsha, Dun Lorezi, and the rest of the lads gathered around and sat down. Tigun started speaking, "How are you all?"

"Good!" everybody answered.

"Any problems?"

"No," everybody answered in unison again.

"I know I promised the mothers of Glosaang that I would take their sons to Elt-duk, but we are going somewhere else now. Under an immediate compulsion, we have to go to the kingdom of Monaar instead of Elt-duk because it is not safe. It is not binding on you to take part in the drills of war. It's not compulsory to go wherever the company is going, but one thing is for sure: this ship is neither going to Elt-duk, nor to Mirkota. If some of you want to stay in the kingdom of Monaar, you may do that and I will request Mr. Parsomin to try his best and send you back to Mirkota. I feel very thankful that you all came here for me. I will try my best to do you good."

A lad stood up and said, "Mr. Tigun, you are our Sharptooth. You supported us when no one was ready to help us. You gave our town a new life and hope. If many of us are alive right now, you are the reason behind it. We will never forget this favour, Mr. Tigun."

"Don't say that, my dear boy," Tigun replied.

"He is right," Doperi said. "It is now time for us to give you all our support. We know you will not do anything wrong." He started chanting 'Sharptooth, Sharptooth, Sharptooth!' and the rest of them joined in too. Doperi then approached Tigun and said, "You don't need to worry, Glosaang is with you."

The lads started shouting, "Hy hord! Hy hord! Hy hord!" and everyone became motivated.

Every morning and evening, they practiced for war. Tigun, Misarel and Parsomin taught them attack, defence, and survival techniques. Parsomin taught defence, while Tigun taught them attack. All the men on Dafort put in their best efforts. Doperi and O'blame engaged in it too. Though they were old, Parsomin wanted them to take part in the drills too.

"You want me to fight at this age too, Tigun?" Doperi asked in anger while grabbing the sword in his hand.

"Yes," Tigun replied and smiled. Doperi smiled back at him.

Almost twenty days had passed and the drills became harder day by day. Not much food was left on the ship now, but Parsomin assured them that they would reach soon. "We will cross the Triangle of Zabaar soon. I recognize the trees there, they are still present in my memories, along with the small mountains of Zabaar," Parsomin explained happily.

"Have you come here before?" Asto asked him.

"Yes, many years ago. I know them and they know me," Parsomin replied proudly and smiled. "The kingdom of Monaar is not very old. I think we should reach there in two or three days."

After two days, the last of their drills got completed. Everyone was tired and sat down on the deck. A light winter had set near Monaar. Hot drinks of falus were served to everyone to heal quickly.

Tigun spoke, "We left Mirkota with the aim to hunt for the unclaimed wealth of Elt-duk, but now our hunt is to claim our place on this mighty Earth, and to save Elt-duk from the devils. We came to rob Elt-duk, but now we have to save it. Are you with me?"

"Yes…we are! Hy hord, Hy hord!" everyone chanted.

"Have your dinner, lads. We will reach Monaar tomorrow."

"He is a true leader," Parsomin said to Doperi. "What do you think Mr. Doperi?" he asked.

"Yes, and he is brave too," Doperi answered.

While everyone was leaving for dinner, Parsomin chased after Asto and called out, "Asto, Asto, where are you going?"

"For dinner," Asto replied.

"Look lad, if you want to see the real beauty of nature, wake up early tomorrow," he told him.

"What kind of beauty?" Asto asked with excitement.

"You will know tomorrow. Now go and have your dinner," said Parsomin and left.

CHAPTER 12

KINGDOM OF MONAAR

The next day, Asto woke up early and rushed to the upper deck from his cabin, thinking that he had gotten too late to see the beautiful scene that Parsomin had told him about. As he came up, he started searching for Parsomin. The sun was yet to rise. He found him at the edge of Dafort.

"Mr. Parsomin, did I miss it?" he asked.

"Miss what?" Parsomin asked.

"The beautiful scene," Asto replied.

"No, it's yet to come, my dear boy. Bardi, give us some tea please."

"Yes, Mr. Parsomin," Bardi replied.

"What is this beautiful scene, Mr. Parsomin?" Asto was very eager to know about it.

"Wait, lad. You will come to know it very soon," Parsomin replied with a smile. After some time, he pointed his finger to the horizon and exclaimed, "Look, lad, at the top!"

Asto looked up at the great entrance of Monaar where the statue of Xera Monaar stood tall.

"I have never seen such a big statue in my life," Asto said

Parsomin smiled at him while drinking his tea. As they entered into Monaar, he said, "Look to your left, Asto. They are the Goldwun trees, thousands of them, with their gold and white leaves. They shine like gold when the sun rays fall on them. Look, the sun has started rising at the horizon. Look at the trees now. In the middle, you will see a natural waterfall. This whole forest is so beautiful. It is called the Peace Forest. Looking at it, you will feel inner peace and beauty everywhere. The kingdom of Monaar is a peaceful kingdom. This forest was created as a peace memorial for the world. They want to give out the message of peace to every traveller that passes by here."

For sometime, Asto watched the beautiful scenic of the Peace Forest continuously.

"Do you like it, Asto?" asked Parsomin.

"Very much," Asto replied. "But we are not going here for peace, am I right, Mr. Parsomin? A war is upon us. Will the Trroths understand this message of peace?" Asto asked.

"You are right, Asto. The Trroths don't want peace," Parsomin said and took a deep breath. "They want revenge and war, but you don't worry. We are together."

Asto smiled and they continued talking and having their tea.

The port of Monaar now came to their sight at a short distance. After sometime, Dafort reached the port. Tigun, Misarel, Doperi, and O'blame all came to the upper deck. Many ships, big and small, were docked at the port. Most of them were trade ships. The kingdom of Monaar exported many things, and traders from many other towns came there to purchase and sell goods. There was already a good rush of people and traders at the port of Monaar.

Tigun, Misarel, and Aaro Zinsha got off Dafort after it was anchored at the port. All of them had touched land after a long time. They looked around, trying to figure out what was going on. Some people were counting boxes, while some were lifting and placing them on big wooden carts. Some were giving instructions to the labours, but on the whole, there was a loud cacophony of people all around. Everyone seemed busy. They were surprised to see such a large crowd so busy at work.

“We have to move,” Parsomin broke the silence. They started walking on the grey-stoned pathway that was beautifully decorated with flowers on either side. They had only walked a little when a guard who had been watching them, stopped them and said, “Where have you come from? Where are you going? Show me your identity papers.”

Tigun and Misarel looked each other. “Look, we...” Misarel start speaking, but Parsomin came to the front and intervened, “They are with me.”

“Mr. Buk Parsomin! After a long time!” the guard exclaimed.

“I think, yes,” Parsomin answered.

I was very young when I saw you the last time,” the guard said and laughed.

“Oh, really? Well, you are not too old yet, lad,” Parsomin said with a smile.

“Yes, Mr. Buk Parsomin. Are all these people with you?”
“Yes, they are all my friends and members of our crew from

that blue ship, Dafort. This is Mr. Bardi. Please help him with everything that he needs," Parsomin replied.

"Sure, sir. Where are you heading?" asked the guard.

"I am going to meet the King. I want to meet him urgently," answered Parsomin.

"How will you people get there?" the guard asked again.

"We will see," Parsomin said.

The guard immediately called his servant forth with a horse cart and said, "Take this, Mr. Parsomin."

Parsomin expressed his gratitude to him and said, "Can you please inform the king that I have arrived, and that I want to meet him urgently?"

"Okay, Mr. Parsomin. I will try to inform the King's guards."

"Thank you, lad," he said and they started their journey towards the King's castle.

"King's castle is quite far. We will have to cross the whole city to reach it, but the city will never give you a chance to ignore it. Tall buildings, beautiful monuments, beautiful gardens, and properly arranged markets adorn the city. Enjoy the view of the city, lads!" Parsomin said.

The city was indeed very beautiful and planned well. All the roads and pathways were neat and clean, the gardens were managed well, all the houses were coloured in mostly yellow and white. These were the official colours of Monaar's kingdom, inspired by the Goldwun trees all around them. In less than two hours, Parsomin, Tigun, Misarel, O'blame, Doperi, Asto, Aaro Zinsha, and Dun Lorezi reached the gate of the King's castle.

It had long towers with thick walls surrounding the main building. The tower tops were gilded in gold. Two layers of walls separated the castle from the entrance. Beyond the entrance gate, there were buildings of food storage and grain silos, then the administration buildings, the armoury, and a royal inn, called The Ruveal. Only the most important officials and guests of the kingdom stayed in it. There were some houses there too, with open and beautiful spaces out front. Beyond the first wall were the military camps and bigger armouries. Castle guards and other soldiers lived and trained here. This section had beautiful gardens in it. Beyond the second wall, the King's own castle started. It was surrounded all over by Goldwun trees and there was strict security all over the place.

"We want to meet King Altreen," Parsomin said to the guard behind the gate.

"You can't meet the King," the guard replied from a small opening in the gate.

"Why?"

The guard remained silent. "I am asking why I can't meet the King?" Parsomin asked again.

Then, an old guard came out of the gate and asked, "What do you want, Mr. Parsomin?"

"I want to meet King Altreen, and it is an emergency," Parsomin replied.

The old guard went back to the gate and spoke with the guard inside, then came back to Parsomin. "Mr. Parsomin," he said, "The king is not here in the castle. He has gone somewhere to the south east. He will come back late in the night, maybe even tomorrow morning."

Parsomin remained silent for a while, then said, “I don’t think the guards will let us in.”

“What do we do now?” Misarel asked.

“We’ll have to find a place to stay till he comes back,” Parsomin replied. “Let’s go.” Soon, they found a local inn near the castle to spend the night at.

The next morning, all of them got ready to meet King Altreen. They reached the castle’s gate again and Parsomin demanded entry, but the guard refused again. Some guards who knew Parsomin arrived at the gate just then. They took his message to the royal guards of the King. After a couple of hours, the King summoned them with respect, and the guards escorted them into the castle.

Right beyond the second wall, there was a long white path with colourful decorative flowers on either side. A castle was pure white with a golden dome at the top of every tower. Colourful birds were chirping in the trees nearby. Looking at them, Ispichu started cooing too. Soon, they reached the King’s hall where King Altreen was sitting on his throne. Some of his officials were also there.

King Altreen looked at them and stood up.

“Parsomin!” he said loudly.

“King Altreen!” Parsomin said and bowed to him. Altreen came forward and grab Parsomin’s shoulders. “How are you?” he asked.

“I‘m good,” Parsomin replied, “How are you? Had you gone somewhere yesterday? Is everything alright?”

“Not really,”Altreen replied. “Come, Parsomin. Meet the Chief of my Army, Myanya. He and his soldiers caught something strange yesterday.”

"What is that?" Parsomin asked eagerly.

"Are these your friends?" Altreen asked, looking at the rest of the group.

"Yes," Parsomin replied.

"Is talking about strange things in front of them safe?"

"They have seen many strange things in the last couple of months. They even saved my life," Parsomin replied.

"What happened to you?" Altreen asked.

"Long story, I will tell you later. You can say what you were going to say."

"Day before yesterday, we heard news of some quarrels in the south-east outskirts of Monaar. However, it was not a mere quarrel. Some of our guards went there to investigate, but only one of them came back alive to report it. What he told us was unbelievable! The guards gave this information to our southern army base. Myanya was there at that time for a regular meeting. Then, he went there with my warriors. Myanya, tell them about it."

'Yes, my King," Myanya replied. "When I reached there, I saw a creature who had wings and legs, but a very weird face. It had claws and sharp canine teeth that could rip anything apart. He had a strong muscular tail too. The creature was flying and fighting with our guards who could barely handle him. He had killed five of our guards by the time I reached there. I have never seen a creature like it in my life before. I ordered my soldiers to attack him, but he lifted two of them up by his legs and threw them down. We then tried a different strategy. Some of us distracted him, while some archers went to a different location to target him, and the plan worked. The arrows hit him and he fell. We brought him to our army base from there."

"The next day, they informed me all about it," said King Altreen. "I reached the base and we called our specialist healers to medicate him. We bound him and tried to save him, but he died nonetheless."

"Burburuks," Parsomin muttered.

"Did you say something?" Altreen asked.

"Burburuks," Parsomin said aloud. "What you caught yesterday was a Burburuk."

"What?" Altreen asked.

"They are ancient creatures, horrible ones too," Parsomin replied.

"How do you know about them?" Altreen asked.

"I fought one of them about two months ago. They almost killed me. That's when these people saved my life." Parsomin motioned towards Tigun and the others.

"That is the reason why I wanted to meet you with such urgency, Altreen," Parsomin answered.

Altreen did not break his gaze from Parsomin "What is going on, Parsomin. Tell me," Altreen asked, a little worriedly.

"I think no information has reached you yet," Parsomin said.

"What information? What do you mean by it, Parsomin?"

"About the danger that is approaching all of Southly Earth. I was assigned to go look for the Als-mites, but we were attacked by Burburuks and I found myself on a mysterious island where my fight with them continued. Luckily, this company of Tigun and Misarel was passing from there and they saw me fighting with the Burburuks. Mr. Tigun Sword Runner bravely convinced the rest of them to come save my life," Parsomin explained.

"But what is the danger? And how many of these Burburuks are there?" Altreen asked.

"The blaze of Elt-duk has started, Altreen. The Trroths wants their old revenge. They want one of their own to rule over Elt-duk as a king. And Elt-duk wants its ruler. They woke up the ancient creatures Burburuks and made them their pets. They are very large in numbers. Men, the Als-mites are in danger."

"What are you talking about, Parsomin? No Trroth has been alive for many centuries. Trroths are a myth. They vanished from Earth centuries ago," Altreen tried to reason with him.

"Am I lying then? What you saw yesterday was a clear proof of it," Parsomin answered Altreen.

Altreen remained calm. "What revenge are you talking about, Parsomin?" he asked after a pause.

"Don't you remember what King Volesalt did to the Trroth's King?"

"Yes, I have heard," Altreen said.

"Altreen, they want revenge from all men, and they have been preparing for it for many decades without raising the slightest of doubt."

"But the Trroths had all vanished," Altreen said.

"No, my King. Some remained. The family of the Trroth King and some other Trroths survived. They hid themselves in the unreachable corners of Southly Earth, from where they grew slowly. All of us, men, Als mites, and saints, forgot about them, but the Trroths always remembered the wrong done to them. El MnDadore, the great grandson of the Trroth King–Aer Draul, never forgot how King Volesalt deceive his great-grandfather. He is the leader of the Trroths now. After King Ballanduall, everyone forgot about Elt-Duk, thinking that nobody was eligible to rule over it, but the Trroths began to occupy Elt-duk then with ferocity and ruthlessness, their eyes burning with the rage of revenge. All the rest of us got scattered, living in our own small kingdoms. Nobody united, therefore the Trroths took advantage of the situation and started to claim Elt-duk for themselves. If we don't unite now, Elt-duk will soon get its new ruler and the rest of us will perish in vain. They will easily occupy the kingdoms of men, as the Als-mites are too weak to help anymore too," Parsomin explained.

While listening to all this, Altreen sat down on his throne and took a deep breath. "It means that a war is upon us?" Altreen asked.

"Yes, King Altreen, son of Wargets. A war is indeed upon us," Parsomin replied. Silence presided over the King's hall.

"What should we do now?"Altreen asked.

"We should prepare ourselves and our soldiers to fight, and alert the other kingdoms as well," Parsomin answered. "We also need to have a plan and a strategy."

Altreen called for a map and everyone gathered around the center table over which the map was placed.

"We should send some troops to Volesalt and the City of Tolesa to alert them of this, as well as help them in case of an early attack. I will go to the Als-mites myself to tell them about the present situation and ask for their help. I will try to bring help from Westly Earth and the other lands too, which may be required if Volesalt breaks and the Trroths march towards the City of Tolesa," Parsomin explained.

Altreen became silent. "What happen, Altreen?" Parsomin asked.

"I don't have enough army to send to two different places at the same time. Leave my city on its own,"Altreen replied.

"I am not asking you to send a lot of people, but they need our help, Altreen! The first attack will be on Volesalt, and then the City of Tolesa. If both the kingdoms are won over by the Trroths, they will point their eyes next upon Monaar," Parsomin said.

"If that happens, Monaar is capable of battling any army alone," Altreen said angrily. Nobody said nothing for a while.

"Look Altreen, both the kingdoms are unaware of the danger. They need our help and ignoring them will be a big mistake, not only for Monaar, but for everyone," Parsomin tried to explain.

"I can send a troop of my army to Volesalt, but not a single man from Monaar will go to the City of Tolesa," Altreen said slowly.

"This is not the time to remember your old quarrels, Altreen," Parsomin said angrily.

"Why not, Parsomin? You know what the people of Tolesa did to my great grandfather and grandfather?" Altreen said.

"I know, Altreen. But this is not the right time to remember all of that. We are all standing on the edge of destruction. If you can save yourself from the Trroths alone, then continue to think about your personal issues," Parsomin said furiously.

"All my life, I have been hearing what the Steward of the City of Tolesa did to my family. They almost wiped out my entire family. Nobody helped them. You know everything, Parsomin. You were there," Altreen said, getting emotional.

"Yes, I was there and I opposed the decision. Your great-grandfather Xera Monaar was a good man and a good friend. He always thought about the betterment of the city and its people," Parsomin replied to Altreen.

"I know it. You and the other saints of Buk din duk helped my grandfather establish this land, and that's why I have huge respect for you, Parsomin," Altreen replied.

"I know, Altreen. This is why you have to believe me when I say that our land is in great danger. Please, send your troops to alert both the kingdoms," Parsomin pleaded with him.

"I am going now, Parsomin. I will tell you what I can do very soon. Till then, you are my guest. Myanya!" Altreen called out. "Take them to the dining hall, then arrange rooms for them at The Ruveal. Take care of everything for them. They are my most special guests. Do you understand?"

"Yes, my King," Myanya replied.

"Parsomin, I really like to talk to you, as I did in my childhood, but time is something very unpredictable. You taught me many things, and I remember some of them," Altreen said to Parsomin, then took their leave.

The group remained standing there for a while, then Myanya came and escorted them out to the royal guests' dining hall. It was a lavish hall with beautiful sculptures of Monaar kings of the past. A big white table was set in the middle with golden veins embossed all over its surface. It was surrounded by white chairs that had golden cushions. All of them got seated there for lunch. The waiters came and started serving lunch to them. It composed of different kinds of bread, spicy potatoes, spinach soup, red tomatoes, black and green grapes, fine roasted red meat, white and yellow sweet balls, and all of it was served with Monaar's locally prepared wine. They started eating and discussing Altreen's decision.

After lunch, the servants came and escorted them to The Ruveal, the royal inn. It was a wide and big space where a beautiful building was constructed. It had a big board out front where the name Ruveal was written very beautifully. It was a white building with maroon coloured detailing. There was an open garden at the middle of the building, with a barn at the back for keeping horses.

"I have never seen an inn so beautiful and big as this," Doperi said.

"It's for King's men only," Parsomin replied.

It had a big entrance with beige coloured stone on the floor and maroon veins embossed on it. Luxury light blue sofas were placed everywhere in the hall which also had a big center table on which beautiful flowers were placed. The King's servants told the innkeeper about the guests, and Parsomin informed him about their belongings which were still at the other inn. The Innkeeper asked his servants to fetch their belongings from there.

The Innkeeper then showed them their rooms which were on the first floor. The stairs led up to a long gallery which held the door to each room and got connected at the end to a large terrace from where the castle was visible.

The rooms were big and luxurious. They contained soft cozy beds with white linens and maroon blankets. Flowers were placed on each table, while the chairs and sofas were neatly arranged in the corners. The walls were white and the floor was covered by beautiful imperial carpets.

"Do you like it, Asto?" Parsomin asked.

"Yes, very much," Asto replied.

"The rooms are beautiful," Misarel said. "We have never seen an inn like this before."

A servant came in just then with tea pots. "Please arrange some chairs on the terrace," Doperi said to the servant.

"Why?" asked Tigun.

"Oh, come on, Tigun. The terrace is beautiful, we will enjoy the view."

Misarel brought out some wooden smoking pipes for Tigun and himself.

"Where is mine?" Parsomin asked.

"You smoke?" Tigun asked.

"In this kind of a situation, yes," Parsomin replied and smiled.

"You can take mine," Tigun said.

"Thanks."

Chairs were arranged on the terrace and tea was served.

Misarel and Parsomin started smoking, while the others had their tea. “What now?” Tigun asked Parsomin.

“Will he send his army or not?” Misarel asked Parsomin too.

“He will. He will not refuse me,” Parsomin replied.

“Misarel, can we go back to Mirkota?” O’blame opened his mouth after a very long time. “There is nothing for us to do here. We are businessmen, not warriors. We almost ruined our biggest hunt on which we had invested many Droshes, and there is no chance of us getting our money back, but we can save ourselves. We can hunt the other lands. We have all invested everything in this hunt, you know it Misarel.”

“Yes, I know,” Misarel replied.

“Don’t you know it, Tigun?”

“Yes, I know it, Mr. O’blame,” Tigun replied.

“Then why are you people making a fool out of yourselves? We are in Monaar now and Parsomin is safe. Why can’t we just leave?” O’blame revealed his inner feelings to them. Parsomin had been listening to everything.

“Asto, Dun Lorezi, Aaro Zinsha, you three can go to your room now,” Tigun said.

“I should also take your leave, as you have matters to discuss amongst yourselves. We will meet in the evening,” Parsomin said and left.

CHAPTER 13

THE CONSPIRACY OF THE STEWARD OF TOLESA

That evening, Tigun, Misarel, Doperi and Asto were sitting on the terrace. Tigun and Misarel were smoking pipe. Parsomin came in and sat on a chair.

"Where's O'blame?" Parsomin asked.

"He is in his room," Misarel said and offered the pipe to Parsomin.

"No, he has left for a walk. I saw him leaving," Doperi replied.

"I think he is looking for Monaar's treasury," Misarel laughed. "Beware, Mr. Parsomin, he might take favours from you against having left you safely in Monaar. He might ask you to create some Droshes for him out of your magic," Misarel said and everybody laughed.

"How old are you, Mr. Parsomin?" Asto asked suddenly.

"For how long have you been wanting to ask me this question?" Parsomin asked.

"Since this afternoon," Asto replied. "Tell us, Mr. Parsomin, how old are you?" Asto asked again.

"Hmm, you know, Asto…I forgot to count my age for the last two or three hundred years, so I don't know," Parsomin replied and laughed out loud.

"Yes, Parsomin. From what King Altreen said, it sounded like you were there when Xera Monaar's family was exiled from the City of Tolesa," Asto said.

"You also said you were good friends with Xera Monaar, which means that you are probably older than a century," Misarel also showed his eagerness to know Parsomin's age.

"But you do not look a 100 years old," Tigun said.

"I told you, I forgot to count my age about two or three hundred years ago. I don't know how old I was even two hundred years ago. Counting my age every year was such a monotonous process, that I did not find it worthy at all after a while. But yes, I was already old when I stopped counting my age. However, I do not remember my exact age."

"Is that true?" Tigun asked.

"Yes, Mr. Tigun."

"But how have you been living for so long?" Misarel asked.

"Age is just a number. I am a saint of Buk din duk. My life is for a cause."

"What cause?" Misarel asked.

"Peace," Parsomin replied, "I have fought many wars to create peace on Earth, to make it a better place."

"Have you ever fought with the Trroths before?" Asto asked.

Parsomin smiled. "No, Asto. Trroths had vanished before I was born. In the last fight, King Volesalt had gotten the

Trroths on his side to fight against his sister, Queen Tolesa. Men and Trroths fought together against other Men. Our saints helped Queen Tolesa, but the Trroths were eventually betrayed by King Volesalt. Men are weak for power, wealth and treasure, so they easily become puppets in the hands of desire. King Volesalt was a sure example of it. He killed his own family for it. All that is going on now is due to what men did centuries ago," Parsomin explained. "You want to know why Altreen was so furious about the City of Tolesa? Xera Monaar, King Altreen's great grandfather was a good man. He was a blacksmith. His arms were famous all over Southly Earth. After the fall of the Queen, the city remained scattered for a long time. It was then ruled by the stewards. Many years of rule corrupted the stewards' minds. Murders for the throne were very common in the City of Tolesa. During their rule, betrayal and deceit was everywhere. People of Tolesa don't like stewards at all.

Lovinzo Dorso became the 12th steward. He was a cruel man. He had snatched the throne by killing the previous steward. He start torturing people. People didn't like Lovinzo much anyway. Xera Monaar was angry with everyday's nuisance due to him like the increment of taxes, weird punishments without crime, etc. He started gathering people against Lovinzo. Other people of Tolesa were also quite angry with him, so they readily joined Xera Monaar. Xera just went up to people and spoke against Lovinzo and his activities. People started following him. Many people even joined Xera Monaar and his small movement against the steward grew bigger. Xera Monaar got many supporters for his little revolution in a very small time. Xera Monaar's house became the center where strategies against the stewards were made. People started liking Xera Monaar because he gave a voice to people's inner feelings. His popularity increased day by day. Spies of the steward sent information about this campaign to Lovinzo. The steward was afraid, thinking that Xera Monaar might challenge his claim over the throne with the help of people. He made a plan to break Xera Monaar's campaign. He sent some of his trustworthy spies to join him so that steward Lovinzo could get regular news about his movement.

The spies joined Xera Monaar's circle. They first started giving him some internal information about the steward's administration, then some other internal news about the castle, introducing themselves as servants of the steward's administration. Thus, they won the trust of Xera Monaar and his fellow men. The spies of the steward became important members of Xera's revolution. Xera Monaar gave them a place in his secret meetings too. The steward had now won half the battle. Secret information regarding the campaign now started coming to steward Lovinzo regularly. For a while, everything went on just like that.

Soon, steward Lovinzo got news that the rebellion was going to start a big armed movement against him, and that they were only waiting for a good chance. Lovinzo understood that it was now time for him to crush this whole campaign. He made a plan to stop Xera Monaar by manipulation, so that he could sentence him to death and make him the culprit.

In a secret meeting, the disguised spies shared that the steward was going west for some time. People of the city agreed that it was the right time to attack the castle. Spies of the steward encouraged Xera Monaar to attack the castle in this time too, assuring him that the soldiers inside the castle were on his side. They promised that they would clear our the path at the castle, so there would be no need of a fight and they would capture the throne easily. Some of the spies, along with the city's people, started chanting Xera Monaar's name loudly, and he agreed to the plan. Xera Monaar's family was quite afraid of the entire ordeal and tried to convince him to not go ahead with it, but he assured them that nothing bad would happen, since the entire city and the castle's soldiers were with him.

When the rebels heard that the steward had left the castle, they decided to attack it the same night. When the time came, almost five hundred men marched on the castle, but not without a lot of arms or weapons since everyone was convinced that the castle's soldiers were with them. When they reached the castle, the soldiers gave them an easy entry. They got in and started rioting inside. Monaar tried to stop them, but they suddenly heard a voice, "You are caught, tiny mouse! Xera Monaar, the people's man." It was the steward's voice. The spies in disguise now revealed their true allegiances and started killing the rebels, as did the castle's soldiers. Unarmed and betrayed, the rebels got easily killed by the soldiers. There was blood-shed in every corner of the castle. Xera Monaar was arrested by the King's guards.

Soon, news spread in Tolesa and the world outside that a rebel movement had been crushed by steward Lovinzo. Everyone knew how cruel Lovinzo was. At that time, I was with the Als-mites. I reached Tolesa with some other saints from Buk din duk. Steward Lovinzo punished Monaar very cruelly and bitterly, then presented him in front of everyone on the streets. His condition was bad.

Lovinzo convicted him for many cases, and wanted a death sentence for him by the city's judiciary, which was run by his men. We opposed the steward's rule and challenged him. We told him that he couldn't take a decision on his own, since he was not the King of Tolesa. The matter had to be taken to the Tri-jury (a jury of Als-mites, Saints and Men). Lovinzo got nervous and frightened, knowing that the tri-jury would surely oppose him. "We tried to set Xera Monaar free, but he didn't release him. We fought with the guards too, but he had taken Xera Monaar to an unknown place. I tried to meet Xera Monaar many times, but he had hidden him. We tried to take Lovinzo to the Tri-jury, but he refused to go each time. Then one day, we took the Tri-jury to Tolesa. The oldest and wisest of the Als-mites, the High Saint of Buk din duk, and a great scholar from the north reached the city. When Lovinzo heard that the tri-jury was about to reach the castle at any moment, he took a cruel step. He killed Xera Monaar and portrayed his death as a suicide. We all became numb. I tried to fight with him, for he had killed an innocent man. The tri-jury left the castle. I was in deep shock still, but Lovinzo didn't stop here. He exiled Xera Monaar's family."

"But why does King Altreen hate the people of Tolesa? Weren't they with Xera Monaar?" Tigun asked.

"When the sentence was given to Xera Monaar, nobody opposed it, and when Lovinzo exiled his family, nobody gave them shelter. He had given his life to Tolesa and to the people of Tolesa, but nobody came to help his family after him," Parsomin said. "Some saints from Buk din duk and I helped them. Brombursson was Xera Monaar's eldest son. He, his mother, and his two younger sisters were with us. We brought them to these lands and built a temporary settlement for the family. There used to be a town here at that time, Guzeva. Not many people lived here. We found that the town was full of minerals and nature's gifts, like adequate water and plantation land, but there was no one to unite the people living here who remained involved only in their own small jobs.

Brombursson was an intelligent and hardworking man who had excellent leadership qualities like his father. He forgot the bad memories associated with his father and only remembered the lessons he had taught him. He united the people of Guzeva to lay the foundation of a kingdom. He turned the resource opportunities in the town into trades of iron ore, weapons, oil, fruits and vegetables. Brombursson promoted art and artists too, and their artefacts became famous. People chose him as their leader. Brombursson had a child, Wargets. Wargets was a good administrator. At only his teenage, he handled most of his father's administrative work. Brombursson handed many jobs over to Wargets. That was the golden period of Monaar. Wargets increased the trade and manufacturing in the city. Officially, Wargets gave the name 'Kingdom of Monaar' to these lands and became the first King of Monaar. Brombursson had been a good leader, but he was a simple man. He didn't declare himself as a King ever. Wargets went on to have one son and two daughters. Now, Altreen, Warget's son, rules the kingdom and he has a young daughter."

Silence hung in the air at the terrace, with only some distracting noises of the wooden smoking pipes. Parsomin stood up and took a few steps forward as he said, "Tigun and Misarel, I know you had invested a great deal in this hunt, and as traders, you require profits so that you may run your houses and families comfortably."

"I am not a business man. I don't understand business, but whatever," O'blame said.

"You people are not warriors, but traders. I brought you all here and that's my mistake, or perhaps it may be your destiny. I know I forced you to come here," said Parsomin apologetically

'But you also saved us from a big danger," Asto interrupted.

Parsomin smiled and said, "I can't give you your money back. Perhaps you can hunt for gold in the other lands. I don't know what will stop the Trroths or how Monaar will react to the situation, but I don't wish to keep any of you bound to this. If you wish to go back, you should. I will be happy for you and bless you for your utmost contribution towards the Earth. I will get things arranged for your journey home. Go, live out your lives with your families. There are many young lads with you, Tigun and Misarel. You are responsible for them all. Choose wisely. I must go now." Saying this, Parsomin left. The rest of them remained seated there for a while, then returned to their respective rooms.

The next morning, Parsomin went to meet them, but no one was in their rooms. He went to the dining hall, were he found Tigun, Misarel, Doperi, O'blame, Asto, Dun Lorezi, and Aaro Zinsha.

"I think the decision has been made," Parsomin said and smiled.

"Come, have breakfast," Misarel invited him.

Parsomin sat down and asked him with a straight face, "So, when will you be going?"

"Soon," Misarel replied. "Will you arrange for the things we would need on our journey, as you said?" he asked Parsomin while biting into an apple.

"Oh yes...yes," Parsomin said and downed a glass of lemon water. After a while, he got up and said roughly, "So you are indeed going?" Without waiting for an answer, he started walking away.

"Parsomin," Misarel called out. Parsomin stopped and turned around.

"Wait! Hear us out," said Misarel. "Yes, we are going, but not to Mirkota. We will travel with you to Southly Earth. We had already decided on that when we were back at Dafort, and our company never goes back on its commitments. We are now the warriors of Mother Earth."

Parsomin's dull face suddenly bloomed. He walked back happily and gave Misarel and Tigun a very tight hug.

"Mr. O'blame, you may go back to Mirkota, if you want," Misarel turned back and said. Everyone turned to look at O'blame. "There is no need to put your own life in danger along with us. We have decided to go to Southly Earth. We know what we promised back in Mirkota. Our agreements, terms and conditions are no longer valid. You have invested more money than us in this hunt, but we are losing just as much as you are, putting ourselves in danger despite the responsibilities that we have on us. Anyone from this group can go back freely, nobody will stop you."

Parsomin went up to Mr. O'blame and said, "I will arrange for your journey back to Mirkota. Till then, you can stay here. I will talk to the King myself."

A man came in just then and interrupted them, "King Altreen wants to meet you all at the King's hall."

Everyone came out of Ruveal Inn and headed towards the castle. They entered the King's hall where King Altreen was sitting with his officials.

"Parsomin!" he exclaimed upon seeing the group and got up. All the other officials followed suit. "Any complaints with my hospitality?"Altreen asked.

"No...not at all," Misarel replied.

"Parsomin, I really wanted to join you yesterday, but an important meeting came up."

"It's okay, Altreen. Once we win this battle against the Trroths, we will feast together and sing victory songs," Parsomin said happily. "Also, we are ready to march now, Altreen," Parsomin said confidently.

"Good! But the news is that Buk din duk is under attack," Altreen said morosely.

"What?" Parsomin asked loudly.

"Yes...my secret sources say that, and it is not a rumour."

"So it begins," Parsomin replied.

"Yes," Altreen whispered.

"Why are we waiting then?" Tigun interrupted. "We should start our march southwards immediately."

"If they are attacking Buk din duk right now, the realm of Ballanduall (Volesalt and the City of Tolesa) will be the next target," Parsomin said.

"We should hurry then," Misarel said.

"Prepare the army, Altreen. We will leave Monaar and march southwards tomorrow," Parsomin said.

"You may leave the castle tomorrow, Parsomin. It will take almost a day to reach our army camp on the southern borders. Myanya will send a message to the army camp today so that they will be ready to receive you when you reach there tomorrow."

"How many men are you giving me?" Parsomin asked.

"How many do you want?" Altreen asked.

"Give me five thousand men. Three thousand will go to Volesalt, and the rest will be sent to the City of Tolesa. After Buk din duk, the next attack will definitely be on Volesalt. We will have time to prepare for war in the City of Tolesa, while your army and the army of Volesalt holds the Trroths there," Parsomin explained. "There is one more thing that I wanted to say to you Altreen," Parsomin said.

"Yes, Parsomin. Tell me," Altreen replied.

"I do not want to forcefully take you and the kingdom of Monaar into this gruesome war, but if Volesalt is defeated, Monaar and Tolesa will have to unite to fight the evil with a combined full strength. I know, this is difficult for you, but for the sake of this world, you'll have to come, Altreen... you'll have to come," Parsomin insisted, grabbing Altreen's hand.

"I will see what I can do," Altreen pulled his hand out of Parsomin's grasp. "If you leave the castle early tomorrow morning, you will reach Monaar's southern borders by nightfall. You can stay at my army camps there. Myanya will go with you till the camps, then he will leave you. The next day, you may start your journey southwards with my army."

"Very well then," Parsomin said.

"Till then, you should arrange for things you'll need on your journey. You will get whatever you people want: weapons, food, animals, whatever. Don't hesitate to ask," King Altreen said.

"We should take leave now," Parsomin said to the rest of them and they started walking out of the King's hall.

"Let's call all our lads here," Doperi said.

"Yes," Tigun replied. "Call them all to Ruveal Inn."

CHAPTER 14

GO BACK ASTO

The party reached back at The Ruveal, took their lunch and came up to their rooms. Tigun stopped at the terrace and sat there on a chair. He spent many hours there, then went to Misarel in the evening. He was thinking about Asto's future through this dangerous journey where death was almost certain. He was frightened for him, and he expressed his feelings to Misarel.

Both of them discussed the matter. "You are right, Tigun. We should send Asto back to Mirkota where he'll be safe and will also alert the others," Misarel said. "It's my fault, I urged you to bring him with us."

"If you knew that our biggest hunt would turn into our biggest war, you would not have asked me to bring Asto along with us," Tigun replied.

"Tigun, it is really dangerous to take Asto with us. There will be ships here at the port of Monaar which will go to Northly Earth. We should send him back on those ships with Mr. O'blame," Misarel suggested. Tigun got up to leave and prepare for Asto's departure.

"Why only Asto, if any other lad wants to go back, he may. There is no shame in it. Their life is just as important," Misarel said to Tigun.

As Tigun started to go, Misarel said again, “Don’t you think, Tigun, that our ship is lost in the middle of the sea?”

Tigun turned around and said exasperatedly, “We ourselves are lost somewhere.”

That night, Asto was all alone in his room when Tigun entered.

“What are you doing, Asto? Did you pack all your things?”

“Almost, Pa,” Asto answered. “We will leave early tomorrow?”

“Yes, we are leaving, but not together,” Tigun answered. “We are departing for the journey of a dangerous war, and you are going home.”

“What? What are you saying, Pa? I am not going home without you.”

“Don’t argue with me, Asto,” Tigun said in a loud voice. “I am doing what is best for you. You are not a warrior. You are just a boy who knows nothing about this cruel world. You don’t know anything about wars and battles.”

Asto remained silent.

Tigun said after a pause, “This battle will not be a small one. This war ensures death, and I can’t let you be here.”

“But Pa, I can’t leave you alone. I will take care of you. I will help you.”

“You don’t worry about me. I can take care of myself. I promised your mother that I would protect you at any cost, and I am doing exactly what is to be done. Pack your bags for Mirkota quietly. Mr. O’blame and maybe some lads are staying here at Monaar till they get a ship back to the North. You will go with them,” Tigun ordered in a loud voice.

Misarel entered the room just then.

"You have to go, Asto. The path we have chosen is not so easy, and you have the responsibility of alerting the people of Mirkota of the upcoming danger," Misarel explained. "They will attack Northly Earth if they succeed in capturing Southly Earth, but we will not let them have Southly Earth so easily, you will see. We will fight them and defeat them."

"I also want to fight with you and defeat them," Asto replied to Misarel.

"Asto, understand this. You have better chances of being safe at Mirkota, and you also have to take care of our family," Tigun tried to explain.

"But you are my family too, Pa. How can I go back if you are in danger here?" Asto interrupted.

"I know...but you have to go. You have to go, Asto. For us, you have to go...try to understand," both Tigun and Misarel put the pressure on Asto.

Asto became quiet as he couldn't say much to both of them. He started packing for Mirkota. Aaro Zinsha and Dun Lorezi came to Asto's room too. "I want to go home, sir," Dun Lorezi said.

"You want to go, Dun Lorezi?" Misarel asked.

"Yes," he replied.

"Okay. You can stay here in Monaar till they arrange a ship for you to go back. Mr. O'blame and Asto are going home too," said Misarel.

Both Dun Lorezi and Aaro zinsha looked at Asto. Asto looked back at them with a straight face. "Aaro Zinsha, what about you?" Misarel asked.

"I will go with the company," he replied.

After this, all of them came out of the room, except Asto. Misarel went to the dining hall for dinner, while Tigun went back to the terrace. Dun Lorezi and Aaro Zinsha were going back to their room, when suddenly Parsomin met them in the corridor.

"Where are Tigun, Misarel, and Asto? Preparing to leave tomorrow?" he asked then.

"Asto is preparing to leave, but not for Southly Earth. He is going back to Mirkota," Aaro Zinsha said.

"What? What are you saying, Aaro? Why is he going to Mirkota?" Parsomin asked, surprised.

"I think Mr. Tigun and Mr. Misarel don't want him to go to Southly Earth," Aaro replied.

"Where are Tigun and Misarel?"

"Mr. Misarel went to have dinner, and Mr. Tigun is on the terrace."

Parsomin went to the terrace where Tigun was sitting and smoking pipe. Parsomin sat next to him. "Why are you doing this, Tigun?" Parsomin asked with some hesitation after a while.

"What am I doing?" Tigun asked.

"Sending Asto back to Mirkota!" Parsomin said.

"I want the safety of my child. That's why I am sending him home, that's it."

"Only your child? The people who came with you on this hunt, trusting you, are they not anyone's children? Many have been killed and many are yet to be killed, are they not the children of anybody? Am I talking to the same Tigun who fought with his friends for a stranger? You are becoming selfish, Tigun," Parsomin said.

"I am not becoming selfish. My son is not a warrior. He has done nothing bad or wrong to the Trroths or anyone else. He is an innocent boy. Why should I guide him into the jaws of death?" Tigun stood up and said.

"Who told you that we're being led into the jaws of death? As long as I am alive, I will be the first one to see death in its face. And remember one thing, Parsomin is not in a hurry to be dead. Besides, Asto is the son of Tigun the Sword Runner, he is a born warrior."

"That's your view, Parsomin. But I know him, he is not cruel. He is a soft hearted boy, and I can't see him as a part of this war," Tigun replied.

"I know how soft hearted he is, but are soft hearted people not warriors? Tigun, you are not able to see his abilities because your eyes are shrouded by a curtain of care and fear!" Parsomin said.

"What happened to you, Parsomin? You agreed to send all of us back to Mirkota this morning because of the danger, if we so wished, and now that I am sending my son back to Mirkota for the same reason, you are arguing with me!" Tigun said in anger.

"Who said that I agreed on sending all of you back to Mirkota?"

"What?" Tigun asked.

"I only said that if you wanted to go, you may go."

"And if we had said yes, then?"

"I knew your answer, I was sure."

"What if we had said yes to going back home?" Tigun asked again.

I would never have let you people go."

"Why?" Tigun asked.

"I need all the goodness on my side in this war, Tigun. You and your company gave this movement a new direction. I was lost, but you and your company saved me and give a new hope to this world."

"So you were lying when you said that we could go home? You are selfish," Tigun replied in anger. "I have decided, Asto will go back to Mirkota and will alert the other towns and cities of Northly Earth, so that they would be prepared."

"Would Northly Earth really be prepared? Would they unite? Northly Earth is scattered, the realm of Prance is scattered, Tigun. You know this very well. They will think him a fool, and will just sit unprepared till something even worse happened. They don't even have an army to fight with the Trroths and the Burburuks," Parsomin said with irritation.

"We will not give the Trroths the chance to reach Northly Earth," Tigun interrupted him.

Parsomin smiled and said, "If you want to defeat the Trroths right here in Southly Earth, don't send Asto back to Mirkota, Tigun. I have already selected the role for him in this war."

"What? What role?" Tigun asked in surprise.

"Yes, Tigun. He has to play a very important role in this journey where he will learn many things. He will have to take many decisions on his own, which will be very beneficial for us...for you. I am sure he will overcome all danger. If you are afraid that he might get harmed, I take the oath to protect Asto. I request you, Tigun, he is required in this war," Parsomin explained.

"You didn't answer me, what role have you selected for him?" Tigun asked again.

"He will be with me on this journey. I know I deserve your skepticism, but I need him to reach the Als-mites. He will be safe with me. I assure you that it will be his journey and he will complete it on his own. You will be proud of him, we will all be proud of him," Parsomin put in everything to convince Tigun.

Tigun sat with his eyes closed for a while. Parsomin approached him and placed his hand on his shoulder. "I promised Asto's mother that I would take care of him. She trusts me. Now you want him to go on without me? Promise me that you will take care of him! Promise me," Tigun said, his eyes swimming with tears.

"I promise you that I will take care of him at all cost. Your promise to Asto's mother will not go in vain, her trust will not break. You have my word," Parsomin replied confidently.

"You can take him with you then," Tigun said slowly, still looking down. Parsomin patted Tigun's shoulder. It was a long night for everybody.

CHAPTER 15

READY TO GO

Early the next morning, Parsomin's voice was buzzing all over the inn. "Everybody ready?" he asked loudly.

Everyone gathered at the terrace. It was still dark as the sun had not risen yet. Tigun, Misarel, Doperi, O'blame, Asto, Aaro Zinsha, and the rest of the lads from Dafort were there now. Tigun came forward and started talking speaking, "How are you all?

"Good," everybody replied.

"Our journey starts here. Back on the Dafort, we pledged to save the Earth. Do you remember?"

"Yes," everyone replied in unison.

"We are safe here for some time, but when we leave the city today and cross the southern borders tomorrow, we will not remain safe anymore. I don't want to threaten, but only alert you because you all are my brothers. If anyone wants to stay here regardless, he may."

"Yes, he may," Parsomin interposed.

"When we cross the borders tomorrow, we will have to face a cruel enemy who wants our life, our everything. They want to kill us, and if we survive anyway, they will want to make us their slaves. If we don't succeed, they will do whatever they want to do with us and our families. But if we unite, we will become stronger. The Als-mites are with us, they will help us in this war."

All the lads started murmuring about the Als-mites at their mention.

"Am I right, Parsomin?" Tigun asked.

Parsomin gave Tigun a strange look, then blinked and said, "Yes, oh yes. They will surely help us."

"Sharptooth…Sharptooth," everyone started shouting. "To the Earth!" Tigun shouted, and everyone followed after him.

Myanya came in just then. "King Altreen is waiting for you at the gate," Myanya said in Parsomin's ear.

We should leave," Parsomin shouted. They started walking and reached the castle's gate. King Altreen was there.

"I think everyone is positive and motivated," Altreen said.

"You didn't have to come here, Altreen," Parsomin said.

"No, I have to. My men are prepared as well. You may cross Monaar tomorrow." He then addressed everyone else, "All of you are heading for a noble cause, but it is dangerous. You may not be the warriors of any kingdom, but you are the warriors of mother Earth now. This will make you stronger than any other warrior."

"Altreen, you should start gathering men. We need you in this war. Monaar is required to participate with its full strength. You will have to come to Tolesa if Volesalt is defeated," Parsomin said to Altreen. Altreen nodded without saying anything.

“Where is Ispichu?” Asto asked.

“He was with you,” Misarel said.

“No,” Asto replied.

“Don’t worry, I sent him free to fly anywhere he wished. He likes Monaar. Maybe he is around here somewhere with his friends,” said Tigun. After a few minutes, Ispichu arrived and perched himself on Asto’s hand.

“There he comes,” Parsomin said and stroked Ispichu’s head. “We should leave now,” Parsomin said. “Altreen, Mr O’blame is staying here for sometime. If any ship goes north sometime soon, he will leave with it.”

“No problem,” Altreen said.

Misarel turned to O’blame and said, “It was nice working with you. We have been together all this while, but our partnership is now ended, although our friendship will remain the same. We are sorry. You were the one who trusted us. You invested many droshes in our hunt, but we didn’t complete it. We have made our choices now, Mr. O’blame, and we have picked different paths. We hope you live safely.”

Everyone shook hands with O’blame and they went their different ways.

“Take care, Parsomin. Take care, everyone,” Altreen said with a smile on his face.

Misarel approached Tigun and said, “I have been meaning to ask you something.”

“What is it?” Tigun asked.

“Why is Asto coming with us?” Misarel asked.

“Long story,” Tigun said.

"Hy Hord! Hy Hord!" all the lads started shouting.

The company started its new adventure with the addition of a new member–Parsomin, and without an old member–O'blame. He and Dun Lorezi had decided to stay at Monaar for sometime till they got a ship to take them back to Mirkota.

Dafort was anchored still at Monaar's port. When Misarel and Tigun asked for Dafort to be sent back to Mirkota, Parsomin refused it, saying that they would need Dafort later.

They started their sprint with the Army Chief Myanya and some other guards towards the southern borders of Monaar where the kingdom's army camp was settled. They had started early and kept a fast pace, and managed to reach the base camp by nightfall. The army was ordered to prepare for a march to Volesalt the very next day. There were many yellow and white tents at the camp which was quite huge in its area. Myanya told them, "It is our southern army base, always prepared for any emergency."

The soldiers were wearing white capes and armours with a hard yellow cloth over it, with a Goldwun tree embedded on it. All soldiers had fine swords and metal shields. All their horses were high bred. Some of the soldiers were practicing for war, while some were cooking or talking to each other. There were bonfires everywhere. When the group had arrived, all the soldiers looked at them, specially Parsomin, very keenly. He was known to some of the older soldiers. They started talking about him.

Arrangements were done for the company in a big tent. All of them assembled together for a meeting where tea and fruits had been arranged for them.

Myanya and company started to make a strategy for their upcoming march. Myanya introduced them to Sebel. "Mr. Sebel is the Commander in Chief of this base, and he will lead the army to Volesalt's kingdom," Myanya explained.

"What about the City of Tolesa? How many men are you sending there?" Parsomin asked.

"We have no orders to send an army to Tolesa," Myanya refused clearly.

"What? But, we talked about this with Altreen. We have to send the army to both the kingdoms at the same time," Parsomin said in anger.

"I have the orders to send an army only to Volesalt," Myanya replied.

"Not good, this is not good," Parsomin said. Nobody said anything for a while. "How many men do you have?" Parsomin asked after a pause.

"Three thousand," Myanya replied. Parsomin sat back quietly, lowering his head. "Fool," he said. "Volesalt is almost six days from here, but we can reach there in five days."

"My army is in good condition. The horses are strong. We can achieve it. My army is ready for the march. We can start tomorrow," Commander Sebel said.

Myanya handed him the official letter of order from King Altreen.

The meeting was over. Sebel and Myanya proceeded to their tents. Myanya warned Sebel to not listen to Parsomin blindly, and to not split their army. Parsomin was still angry with Altreen because he had not listened him. All the rest of them relaxed and waited for the next morning.

CHAPTER 16

THE FIRST CLASH

The next morning, the army camp was buzzing with activity. As everybody woke up and assembled together, Parsomin commanded, "Prepare! We will leave Monaar today. Quickly."

When Parsomin came out of the tent, Sebel asked him, "Mr. Parsomin, are you ready?"

"Yes, I am."

"And what about your friends?"

"I am sure they are too," Parsomin replied.

Outside the tent, almost three thousand men stood ready with their horses, swords, shields, bows, arrows, spears and horse carts loaded with supplies like food and tents. "We have to march today, lads," Sebel shouted loudly. "Is there any fear in you, or do any of you wish to say something?" Sebel asked.

"No, sir," every man in the army replied.

"Our enemy is very dangerous. Are you ready?"

"Yes," everyone shouted loudly. Tigun and the others came out of their tent too.

"Start!" Sebel shouted loudly, and the army of Monaar started its journey towards Volesalt with the company. The thundering clop of their horses and marching feet could be heard from afar. "Grab speed!" Sebel ordered loudly.

The army was achieving its targets efficiently within the time intervals. On the third day, they had completed almost half of their run. The terrain was sandy and the sun was at the zenith.

"Mr. Sebel, how long have you been serving the King for?" Parsomin asked.

"Almost twenty years," Sebel replied.

"Good enough," Parsomin replied.

"I have heard some of your stories," Sebel told Parsomin.

Tigun and Misarel were riding alongside Parsomin, while Asto, Doperi and Aaro Zinsha were right behind them. Ispichu remained perched on Asto's shoulder.

"Oh, really? What have you heard, Mr. Sebel?" Parsomin asked.

Suddenly, something came flying down from the sky, grabbed a soldier with his horse, raised him up in the air and slammed him back down. He almost died from the impact, getting caught under the horse's weight and having something sharp poking into him. Everyone was shocked with this sudden incident.

"Everybody, look up!" another soldier shouted out.

Everyone's gaze darted upwards, as the thing came back again and tried to lift another soldier up with its claws.

"Burburuks!" Parsomin shouted. "Save yourselves! Archers be ready!"

The archers started firing arrows at the Burburuk who was trying to lift up the soldier. He fell down wounded. Almost immediately after, about fifteen Burburuks came down from the sky and started attacking the army.

"Archers, fire!" Sebel ordered.

Asto hid Ispichu in his small bag quickly. Tigun, Misarel, Doperi, Asto and Aaro drew out their swords, while Parsomin drew out his big and long axe. Parsomin yelled, "Make a circle, Tigun. Hurry!"

All of them formed themselves into a circle, while the archers continued to shoot arrows at the Burburuks. They managed to take down almost four Burburuks, while the rest went on to lift the soldiers up in the air with their claws, tail and teeth, then slam them back down. A Burburuk attacked Tigun and he tried to strike it back, but the Burburuk dodged it. Misarel managed to strike one too and scarred its wing, making it scream in anger. It came down again to swoop Misarel off his horse, but Parsomin came in just in time and chopped its wing off with his axe. It slammed down to the ground, screaming loudly. Tigun stabbed his sword into its heart, killing it instantly.

"Lads, cover your sky," Parsomin shouted loudly. Suddenly, arrows started flying over the soldiers.

"Archers, come forward," Sebel ordered. The Burburuks were still attacking. Again, some arrows came flying and hit some of the soldiers.

"Who are they?" Tigun asked.

"Some horses are coming this way," Sebel answered.

"Men? Why are men attacking us?" Misarel asked.

"They are not men," Parsomin said.

"What?" both Tigun and Misarel asked together.

"They are Trroths," Parsomin said gravely, looking at both of them.

"Fire the arrows!" commanded Sebel. The archers shot a hundred arrows at a time. Some Trroths fell down, while the rest kept running towards the army. They were approaching them swiftly, and were now fully visible in their large number.

Everyone was seeing Trroths for the first time in their life. They looked just like men from afar, but when they drew closer, their distinction became more visible. With a light green coloured skin, they seemed as if born out of moss. Their hands and legs were well built and muscular. They all had strong jaw-lines and pointed front teeth with even sharper and longer canines that made them look all the more scary. Their ears were very small, their eyes were fiery yellow, their noses were a little unbalanced, and they all had a distinctive white curved horn growing out of the middle of their bald heads.

They wore black hand guards and gloves, and long black boots. Some of them had naked swords without shields in their hand, while some had bows and arrows which they were shooting from afar.

"Are they really Trroths?" Commander Sebel asked Parsomin, while Tigun, Misarel, Doperi, Asto and Aaro looked at them dumbfounded. Sebel's question dragged them out of their hypnotic state and they turned to look at Parsomin.

"Yes, they are," Parsomin replied. "Tigun, Misarel and Doperi, cover Asto and Aaro! Don't come to the front now," he ordered.

Everybody could smell their awful odour as they drew closer. Parsomin rushed to the front of the line with his horse. “Don’t be afraid, lads,” he called out as he rode. “They are not any more powerful than us. Do not be afraid to face them. Just remember how horrible the enemy is, he shall die by our sword. Our arrows have already killed some of them,” he encouraged them. “Charge!” he yelled, and all the soldiers started to ride speedily towards the Trroths. Arrows were flying from both sides.

Men and Trroths finally clashed. Swords collided with swords, there were screams everywhere. The Trroths were not many in number, but the Burburuks were helping them from the sky. The first battle between Men and Trroths of the third age had started. Soldiers and Trroths were falling like nine-pins. Parsomin and Sebel killed many Trroths, while the Trroths and the Burburuks also killed some soldiers. The archers targeted the Burburuks and managed to kill all of them by the end. Not many Trroths were left now. A Trroth pulled out a horn made of black wood and blew into it. All the remaining Trroths stopped fighting immediately and started rushing back in the direction where they had come from.

“They are receding,” Sebel shouted.

All the soldiers shouted loudly, “TIMO–ABOODA!” (*We are power, and power is us.)*

Parsomin celebrated with the soldiers too. Tigun then approached Parsomin and Sebel. “They are gone, we killed many Trroths today,” Sebel said with pride.

“I think those were only the spies of the Trroth army and were not prepared,” Parsomin said. “But it is a start, and we won our first battle!” he said loudly and everybody started cheering. "We should set up base here. We need to cure the injured and bury our martyrs."

"REST!" Sebel shouted to the army. "We shall make our base here," he shouted again.

Some soldiers started to install the tents. Doperi, Asto and Aaro helped them too. Some of them were engaged in carrying back the dead bodies of their fellow soldiers, and arrangements were made for burying them. Parsomin, Sebel, Tigun and Misarel remained standing there to honour and respect them.

Tents were installed and all the injured soldiers were brought in.

"Doperi, you are required now," Parsomin said.

"I am honoured," Doperi replied. He went into the tent with his bag of medicinal herbs, and started treating the injured.

That night, a bonfire was lit alongside the tents. Parsomin, Sebel, Tigun, and Misarel sat around it, smoking their wooden pipes, while Doperi was busy treating the injured soldiers. Asto and Aaro were resting too.

"It all happened so fast," Tigun said.

"Yes, I had not expected to face the Trroths and the Burburuks so early on our journey. It means that our enemy has an eye on us," Parsomin replied.

"We have to reach Volesalt soon," Misarel said.

"Yes, we do," Sebel answered. "We can start early in the morning, so our injured soldiers will have had a good night's sleep and enough time to heal properly," Sebel said. Parsomin remained silent.

"I can't continue on this journey to Volesalt with you all," Parsomin said after a pause.

"What?" the rest of them asked, surprised.

"Yes, please don't take it any other way. As I told you, I was not expecting this. I thought we had more time, that when we reached Volesalt, we would get a chance to explain our plans and strategies to King Gleemund of Volesalt, and draw him out of his inattentiveness towards this. I have heard he is lazy."

"Yes, indeed he is," Sebel said.

"After that, I had planned to go to the Als-mites and seek their help. Their help and counsel is our utmost requirement right now," Parsomin continued.

"What?" Sebel asked. "You are going to the Als-mites? God's men? Will they help?"

"I think so," Parsomin answered. There was silence between them for some moments, then he continued, "Although under the current situation, I think I will have to go to the Als-mites from here itself. We can't delay it anymore."

"I have heard they live far away from all the other lands and Hovelwoods, not in reach of men. It might take many months," Sebel said.

"Commander Sebel, I am a saint of Buk din duk and I know a secret path that lies in the dark forest which will lead me to Corga forest's far edge. That is close to where the Als-mites now reside. I will reach there soon, don't worry about it," Parsomin explained. "Tigun, I hope you remember what we had decided at Monaar. Asto will go with me."

“What? Why?” Misarel asked surprisingly.

“I can’t answer that now, Misarel. I need him on this journey,” Parsomin explained.

“But Parsomin, it is dangerous to send Asto alone,” Misarel said.

“Asto will not be alone, Misarel. I shall be with him You don’t need to worry about him. We both shall meet you soon, and come back with great help. Stay away from unnecessary fear, it will only lower the power of your mind,” Parsomin said confidently. “I need Asto to go with me. We shall leave tomorrow and ride towards the dark forest in the east.”

“I think Parsomin is right. We need the help of Als-mites in this dreadful war,” Sebel interposed.

“But then, how will we introduce ourselves to King Gleemund?” Misarel asked.

“You will have to make him believe you. Tigun, Sebel, you and our entire army of thousands are witness to the devil’s madness and the start of a cruel war,” Parsomin replied.

“I don’t think he will trust us without you,” Tigun said.

“You don’t need to worry about that,” Sebel said. “I have received King Gleemund on his official visits to Monaar in the past. The duty of receiving him was always given to me, since I am in command of Monaar’s southern army. He knows me very well. Also, I have an official letter from King Altreen to show to the King of Volesalt.”

“Very good, Commander Sebel,” said Parsomin happily. “All right then, it is decided. You all shall continue your journey towards Volesalt, while Asto and I will head to look for the Als-mites tomorrow,” he said and all of them stood up to return to their tents.

The next day started with a cold dawn. Parsomin lay awake, as he hadn't slept the entire night. He went to Asto's tent where Tigun, Misarel and Aaro were also sleeping.

"Asto, Asto!" Parsomin called out quietly. Asto did not budge. "Asto," he called again, nudging him a little this time and succeeding in waking him up. "We have to go," Parsomin said.

"Are the others not going?" Asto asked, still half-asleep.

"Yes, they will."

Asto didn't know the new plan yet. He started to get ready. The rest of them woke up in time too. Asto grabbed all his belongings and put them in his bag. The buzz of activity outside emerged as the sun rose above the horizon. Sebel and Doperi stood waiting outside. Tigun and Parsomin told Asto about the new plan. Asto was somehow not convinced to leave Tigun's side, but Parsomin made him understand the need and his requirement on this journey to find the Alsmites. He cleared all his doubts and convinced Asto to go with him. Tigun, Parsomin, Asto and the others come out of the tent.

As the time for them to leave approached, everyone came near Asto.

"Take care, Asto," Tigun said. "Always wear our forefathers' stone around your neck, it will help you in every situation. Don't be afraid. The situations might test you, but you have to succeed. I may not always be there with you, but my wishes and your mother's wishes are always with you."

"And I will always be with him," Parsomin promised and Tigun nodded. "Why don't you give him the tooth of

Sharptooth that you are wearing around your neck, Tigun?" Parsomin suggested innocently. Both Tigun and Asto looked at the tooth. "I think it will bring Asto good luck and help him fight the dark powers," Parsomin said again with the same innocence.

Tigun took it off from around his neck and gave it to Asto on Parsomin's word. "Wear it, Asto. It will protect you," Tigun said.

"You take care, Pa," Asto said, his eyes growing wet. "Uncle Misarel, you have to take care of both of you."

Tigun's eyes swam with tears too as he hugged Asto. Then, Misarel and Doperi hugged Asto too. "Take care," Asto said to them both. He shook hands with and hugged Aaro Zinsha.

"We will miss you," they told him.

Asto caressed Ispichu's head and said, "Take care of him, Pa."

Both Asto and Parsomin mounted their horses.

"We will see you people soon," Parsomin said. "Go to Volesalt quickly and give them our message. Fight with your full strength. God is with us, God's men will be with us. Help will surely come soon. Have faith in me. Have faith in God. Have faith in yourself, my dear friends. Take care, all of you," he addressed them all before starting to ride eastwards with Asto in the direction of the dark forest.

"Take care, Asto," Aaro shouted after them while running towards them.

Two more members of the company had now diverted their path from the group. It seemed as if the company was getting shorter by the day.

Parsomin had a big responsibility on his head now. Along with Asto, he was headed on a quest to find the Als-mites, where many surprises were waiting for them both. Some problems and some harsh decision making awaited them. The rest of them continued on their journey towards the kingdom of Volesalt, as per their plan to alert them and make preparations for their first big upcoming battle against the Trroths and the Burburuks.

About the Author

Yash Sharma was born in Kota, Rajasthan–the city renowned for its medical & engineering studies, but he didn't follow suit. Instead, he choose commerce and carved out his path in this field, not wanting to continue with Maths and Science as his subjects of study. He has been working in the real-estate sector for the past five years, but has gained experience in various domains and areas of work before, not wanting to be tied down to just one.

He loves outdoor sports, football being his favourite. He holds a special interest for writing and has penned down multiple short stories and poems before.

You can reach him at:

Facebook: @ *eltduk*

Instagram: @ *eltduk*

E-Mail: @ *yash1done@gmail.com*